A VALENTINE'S DAY TREAT

TWO SHORT STORIES

SAM MARIANO

D1364846

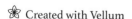 Created with Vellum

THIS VOLUME CONTAINS:

Stranded on Valentine's Day

(The Stitches universe, featuring Griff, Moira, and Seb.)

It's Valentine's Day in Philly, and everything is going wrong. Seb and Griff are stuck at the club, and Moira's car leaves her stranded. Will their first Valentine's Day together be a success, or a miserable failure?

A Perfect Valentine's Day

(*A Morelli family short story.*)

Mateo Morelli just wants to enjoy a quiet Valentine's Day with his wife and newborn daughter. Dinner plans forgotten, baby sleeping peacefully, it seems like he may get his wish... until his eldest daughter turns up missing.

(Also included: a never before seen—but much requested—sexy deleted scene from Last Words.)

AUTHOR'S NOTE

Happy Valentine's Day!

I've been hearing from my readers that they're already missing the characters from my most recent releases, so I decided for a special Valentine's Day treat, how about a short story featuring them?!

It was sensible to pair these couples—er, relationships? Technically, I guess Sebastian, Moira, and Griff are a throuple? At any rate, fans of my primary Morelli couple are also likely to enjoy the dynamic of my *Stitches* throuple, so I put them together in this volume, assuming they have a good number of crossover readers. If you only want to read one or the other, cool, but there's a story for each. (There is also a much-requested Morelli deleted scene, so Morelli readers get a bonus!)

These are not standalone reads. Given they are shorts, it's expected that you already know the characters, their histories, and their dynamics from reading their stories. Both of these short stories take place after the conclusion of the books the characters live in, so obviously reading them first would be ALL the spoilers, and probably a bit confusing. This is bonus content for people who have already read the books. If you try to read this without having read the books, you'll very likely be lost.

Special thanks to Daisy for naming Julia. <3

So, if you're here by mistake, the reading order before this treat is: Stitches, then *Stranded on Valentine's Day*.

And: Accidental Witness, Surviving Mateo, Once Burned, Family Ties, Resisting Mateo, Coming Home, Last Words, and Entrapment... then *A Perfect Valentine's Day*. Many of my readers lamented not getting to see Mateo with his youngest daughter, since her conception happened after the final deleted scene in Entrapment. So, here you go. :)

STITCHES

STRANDED ON VALENTINE'S DAY

GRIFF

I thought my days of mopping floors were far behind me, but on this cursed Wednesday evening, literally everything is going wrong. The morning shipment came an hour ago, so nothing is put away. Our flaky-as-hell Wednesday night closer has taken flakiness to a whole new level; she called twenty minutes ago to tell us she can't come in because her ex-boyfriend surprised her with an engagement ring and she's flying back to California with him—tonight. Now, while the manager scrambles to find someone who will cancel their Valentine's Day plans to come to work, I'm cleaning up a puddle of... I'm not even sure what liquid that a customer left behind on the floor by the bar.

I should probably sterilize the fuck out of his stool, too.

"Kendra laughed for a solid minute and then said no," the manager announces, hanging up from his most recent attempt.

Fantastic. I can't justify leaving them short on a night I already know is going to be busy as hell, but I also don't want to be stuck here on Valentine's Day, of all fucking nights. As it stood, I needed to cut out early today so I could stop and pick up Moira's present and some flowers.

Now it's looking like I won't make it home at all. Seb's damn sure not going to volunteer to stay and give up his plans with Moira.

"Did you try Julia?" I ask.

"Yep, I tried her first. She's usually good for last minute call-ins, but she can't do it; she has a date tonight."

Suddenly there's another, stronger presence on the floor. The man who commands any room he walks into—my best friend and partner, Sebastian St. Clair.

Dammit, Pete. Seb wasn't even supposed to stop in tonight. I could have damn well handled this mess myself, but now my best friend's familiar voice rings out behind me as he takes the situation in hand. "I'll call Julia. Is shipment still in the back?"

The manager nods his head.

Seb lifts his chin, indicating the back room. "Go put it away."

"But we don't have coverage on the bar."

"I'll hang out behind the bar until Julia comes in. Believe it or not, I know how to pour a drink."

Hesitating, the manager considers whether or not he wants to repeat himself, even though Seb clearly heard him. Making the wrong choice, he says, "I already called Julia."

Seb stares at Pete for the beat of maybe three seconds and somehow shrinks the man where he stands. "I have ears, don't I? I know *you* called her. I said *I* will call. She'll come in if I call."

"She has a date."

Sighing, Seb shakes his head and walks around the bar. "She'll cancel the date. Just go put the goddamn order away, Pete. Jesus Christ."

I smirk as a confused Pete heads to the back. When I glance over at Seb, he's already behind the bar, peeling his suit jacket off

2

and rolling the sleeves of his dress shirt up to the elbow. "Look at you, working behind the bar again," I remark.

"I wouldn't get too cocky over there; you look like the janitor." Dropping his gaze, Seb punches in a few numbers and places his cell phone to his ear, grabbing a cloth and wiping down the bar top before we get busy.

I can hear his machinations so clearly as Julia answers the phone and his voice drops to a playful, somewhat intimate tone. "Hey. How's my favorite employee doing tonight?" He pauses for her to answer, smirking even though she can't see him. It comes through in his voice, the charming bastard. I can't even hear her side of the call, and I practically feel poor Julia getting flustered across the city.

"Oh yeah?" he continues. "That sounds like fun. Here's the problem. I *really* need you tonight. Whitney bailed on us; I'm all alone at the bar, poor Griff's over here mopping floors. Pretty sure Pete's going to have a coronary from all the stress. Now, I know he said you had some sort of *date* tonight..."

He pauses, giving our poor, awkward, lovestruck employee just enough time to soak up his words, and the way he trailed off.

"... *But* I was hoping if I asked you as a personal favor, maybe you could do this for me? I mean, you and this jackass can get dinner tomorrow, right? Tell you what, your date tomorrow? It's on me. I wanna buy you that dinner. And the restaurants will be less crowded then anyway. You'll have a nicer evening if you go out tomorrow, plus you can help out your favorite boss. It's a win-win."

I shake my head, sinking the mop into the water bucket, then squeezing it out one more time so I can sop up the last of the water on the floor.

"You can?" he asks, theatrically relieved. "Aw, Julia. You really are my favorite, you know that? Thank you so much."

Now that he's got what he wanted, he ends the call and slides

3

the phone back into his pocket. His tone returning to normal, he tells me, "Bar's covered. Julia will be here in a half hour."

"You are a sociopath," I inform him.

Appearing surprised, he clutches his heart. "That hurts, Griff."

"You know that poor girl has a crush on you and you just took advantage of it to ruin her night."

"It was hers or ours," he states, practically. "You want to disappoint Moira? See, I'd rather coax Julia into rescheduling her date that isn't going anywhere anyway, and you and I can go home to our wife. But hey, if you'd rather stay here and tend the bar all night so Julia can eat fucking burritos with a pimple-faced dipshit, be my guest."

"You are the worst."

"I'll buy her dinner tomorrow. It'll make her month. I'm practically a prince." Nodding toward the back, he goes on without missing a beat. "When you take that mop bucket to the back, you want to tell Pete I got it covered? For some reason he seemed to lack faith in my abilities."

I finish running the mop over that area of floor, dunk it back into the water, and begin to wheel it to the back. As I pass the bar, I casually mutter, "Satan."

Unconcerned, Seb replies, "You'll thank me later when— instead of staying here all night and being a hero—you're relaxed on our couch and Moira's sucking your dick."

Damn, I hate to be an asshole, but that *does* sound a hell of a lot better.

Seb has been here less than five minutes and the entire catastrophe of today is pretty much handled. Pete relaxes when I tell him the bar is covered, Seb tends bar like the old days when we were saving up every dime we could make, and I sanitize the hell out of this stool.

I think I got the shit end of this stick.

A buzzing in my pocket interrupts the miserable string of complaints running through my head. I pull out my phone and see Moira's name flashing across the screen. My whole being lightens and a little smile tugs at my lips as I hit the green button and put the phone to my ear.

"Hello, beautiful," I answer.

"Hey, baby," Moira says, warmly.

I lift my shoulder to hold the phone while I maneuver this stool out of the corner. "What are you up to?"

Moira sighs heavily. "Well, that's kinda why I was calling. I'm in a jam and I was hoping you could help me."

I drop the stool and straighten. "Help you with what?"

"I'm stranded," she tells me. "I was out running the last of my Valentine's Day errands, but now my car won't start. I was hoping if you weren't too busy, maybe you could come pick me up? I'm stuck in this stupid parking lot, I still need to make one last stop, and now I'm running super behind."

I check the watch on my wrist to see if a half hour has passed yet, but to be honest, I'm not even sure why. If Moira needs me, I don't care if the club is covered. The club could literally be engulfed in flames, and if she called me for help, I would drop the fire extinguisher to go help her, even if she only needed help opening a fucking pickle jar.

"Yeah, I can come get you. Did you call Seb?"

"No. I called you."

A shit-eating grin splits my face. Pete may have called Seb, Moira may call him 9 out of 10 times, but Moira needed help today and she called *me* first. "All right, good. Give me a minute to wash my hands and tell Seb I'm leaving. Text me where you are and I'll be right there."

"I'll be waiting. Thank you," she adds, sweetly.

Relief and pleasure mingle together in my bloodstream as I

slip the phone back in my pocket. I can't remember what I was so annoyed about a minute ago, but now I hurry up and get shit sorted so I can get out of here.

I head out to the bar, and sure enough, Julia is behind the counter mooning at Seb. It hasn't even been a half hour, so she must have hung up and made a beeline for her car. Probably canceled her date during the drive here.

I shake my head.

Poor, misguided girl. I know how that unrequited infatuation bullshit goes—and unlike me, she doesn't have a shot in hell of ever getting reciprocation out of hers. Seb would never hurt Moira, not in a million years. He may have lightly toyed with Julia to get her to come in, but that's just what he does. When the situation calls for it, he won't hesitate to step on people if it means he gets what he wants. Since he ruined this poor girl's night so he could go home to his wife, he takes pity on her now and doles out a few minutes of his attention.

Until I walk by, then he holds up a hand. She's been around him just enough that she stops talking mid-sentence. His high-handedness should annoy her, but I swear the adoration in her eyes intensifies instead. Seb abandons her there and approaches the counter, leaning over and meeting my gaze. "Where are you going?"

"Moira called. Her car won't start. I told you I thought it was making a weird noise. We should've had it checked out instead of letting her drive around in the damn thing."

Seb rolls his eyes. "It wasn't making a noise. I took it for a drive after you said that. The noise was in your head."

"Well, now the car has left her stranded in a parking lot in the middle of God knows where, so maybe you should consider the possibility that you're wrong."

"Seems unlikely," he says, lightly.

6

Julia mirrors his posture, leaning her elbows on the counter beside him. "What are we talking about?"

I look Julia straight in the eye. "Seb's wife."

Julia has the grace to flush and look away.

Seb smirks at me. "Well, what are you wasting your time talking to me for, then? Go rescue Moira from the parking lot."

"Don't be an asshole," I tell him, leaving the bar and heading for the door.

"I've tried," he calls after me. "It was too hard."

Moira opens her car door and steps out as soon as she sees me pull into the parking lot. Her long dark hair blows in the wind, whipping around her beautiful face. I'm relieved to see a smile touching her cherry-red lips. On the way over, I worried she might be upset—I think it's a silly thing to be upset about since guys don't really care about Valentine's Day, but she's adamant about making the day nice for us. Of course, she's adamant about making *every* day nice for us, so I probably shouldn't be surprised.

"Thank you so much for coming," she says, grabbing bags out of her backseat. "I need you to take me to—I don't know, a drug store? I need to buy a lipstick."

I blink at her, taking the bags from her and transferring them into my backseat so she doesn't have to. "Lipstick? All this over some lipstick?"

Flashing me a smile over her shoulder, she says, "Well, no, I needed a ride home anyway. I already finished most of my errands, just two stops left."

"Two stops for lipstick?"

"Hopefully just one stop for lipstick," she corrects. "I need a specific shade of pink."

"Whatever you say."

Smiling, she leans in and pecks me on the lips. "That's the spirit."

I catch her around the waist since she's so close. She sways right back into me, looping one arm around my neck and settling one on my side. "I didn't get to give you a proper hello."

"Mm, can't have that, now, can we?" she murmurs, pulling me close as I bend to give her a much better kiss than the peck she gave me. Moira closes her eyes, sighing against my mouth. It's hard to believe I've had her almost a whole year, and it still feels just like it did the first time I was allowed to kiss her. Fucking incredible.

Her blue eyes glow with warmth when I finally pull back. "Well, hello, handsome," she says, teasingly.

I just smile, smack her on the ass, and tell her, "Give me your keys, minx."

Her smile slips a little. "For what?"

"I'm gonna see if I can get your car started."

Moira shakes her head, heading to my passenger side door and opening it. "I already told you, it won't start. There's no time to mess with it. My lipstick awaits!"

So, I drive around Philly looking for the right fucking pink lipstick. Can't say I mind. It's a nice ride with Moira, hearing about her day, telling her about mine. Mostly I just love that I'm the one she called. Seb is always the problem solver—big or small, he's the fixer. Even though this is something small, it makes me happy. I love being there for Moira when she needs me. She's what I need every single day.

"Oh, my God, Griff, look at this."

I'm glancing at shelves of candy at the third drug store when it hits me that in my haste to get to Moira in her time of need, I did not get a chance to pick up her gift and some flowers. Fuck. Now she's with me and I don't know what I'm going to do. I didn't want to take her with me to the store; I wanted to show up and surprise her.

Much as I hate to, I draw out my phone and text Seb. "Hey, can you do me a favor when you leave work?"

"Griff," Moira says again, peeking her head around the corner to see what's keeping me.

"Coming," I reply, dutifully meandering into the aisle where she is.

A delighted Moira holds up a giant gray teddy bear. It holds a big red heart that reads "Happy Valentine's Day!" and has the year embroidered on its foot.

I cock a skeptical eyebrow. "That's what you're getting Seb?"

Moira rolls her eyes at me. "Of course not. We have to get this for Layla. It's bigger than she is. She'll love it."

"Or she'll be terrified of it," I suggest, flipping over the price tag to check. It's an old instinct; I certainly don't need to check price tags anymore, but I've never managed to shake the habit. "We can get it for her, if you want to."

"It's so cute," she gushes, smiling at the bear like it's her niece.

She's gonna make the best mom.

I can't help moving closer, bracing my hand on the small of her back, and pulling her in for a tender little kiss. "You get excited over the weirdest shit."

"I do not."

"You do. It's cute."

Wrinkling her nose up at me in feigned displeasure, she takes her teddy bear and her pink lipstick and heads for the cash register.

9

When we get out to the car, I put Moira's bag in the back seat with all the other shit. Jesus, this is a lot of stuff for Valentine's Day. Isn't this the card and candy holiday? I mean, obviously you buy your wife some jewelry or something, but she's the wife—all she needs to do is show up.

"What *is* all this shit?" I ask, opening a bag to peek in.

Moira reaches back and swats my hand away. "No peeking. That stuff is for you, too. Come on, we still have one last stop to make. The steaks are never going to be done by the time Sebastian gets home," she laments.

"You should not be cooking on Valentine's Day," I tell her, shaking my head. "That is the absolute height of bullshit. We should be taking you out."

"I hate going out to eat on Valentine's Day," she says. "There are people crammed into every corner of every restaurant. You can't even hear yourself think, let alone have a private dinner. I much prefer all of us eating at home tonight, watching a movie, and then going to bed early so I can give you both your presents," she adds, smirking at me.

My cock stirs, recognizing the promise in her words. Still, I can't resist messing with her. "Bedroom presents, huh? We get those types of presents every night."

"Yes, well, you're lucky men," she informs me primly.

I can't help smiling. "Damn right we are."

10

Turns out I am the lucky one, because her last stop is at a lingerie store. She already picked out my "present" and she informed me that she needs my help picking out Sebastian's.

I would say it's a special kind of torment, making me watch her prance around the private dressing room, modeling lingerie she's planning to wear for another man—but it's not, because even if it's for Seb, I'll be there enjoying his present right along with him.

This one is pale blue lace that adheres snugly to every perfect inch of her body. Even after a year with her, my heart is in my throat as she struts toward me. She kept on the nude heels she was wearing with her outfit, and she has one hand on her hip, an adorably cocky little smile on her beautiful face. This woman knows exactly what she's doing to me.

"What about this one?" she asks, turning around, then swiftly bending down and giving me a view to die for—her ass, scantily covered by blue lace. I can see the path to paradise right in front of me. I want to grab her hips, drag her little ass back against me, and bury my face in that beautiful pussy. Someone needs to teach her a lesson for being such a tease. I should eat her out right here in this fucking dressing room and see how quiet she can be.

Since she knows I can't do that, she shoots me a saucy smile and slowly straightens. "Did you see the bra?" she continues, moving even closer and doing the meanest thing ever—straddling my lap, lowering herself and brushing against the raging arousal I'm shifting to accommodate.

"I did," I murmur, thickly.

Moira brings her delicate hands up her sides, then over her breasts, cupping them and giving them a gentle squeeze. "Wanna feel?"

I narrow my eyes at her, grabbing her hips and holding her

against me while I rock my erection between her legs. "I already feel about all I can handle in public, sweetheart."

She grins, leaning in and brushing her lips against mine as she murmurs, "Good."

If she's as sexually frustrated as I am, I can't tell. She pops up off my lap and heads for the dressing room. "I'll be right back to show you the white one."

"Why don't we just buy all of them?" I suggest, as she walks into the dressing room. "I can say with a high degree of certainty that we will both love all of them."

"I was already planning on it. I just like teasing you," she says, honestly.

Can't say I don't like when the little minx teases me, so I guess I have to stay put and ride out this hard-on while she parades around in another tiny scrap of see-through fabric.

I can hardly think straight by the time we leave the lingerie store. Moira is still prattling on about steak, and the last thing I want to deal with when we get home is cooking. After all the torture she just put me through back there, I need to haul her in the house, drop all the bags, and drag her to the bedroom so I can sink my cock inside her and fuck out all this frustration.

To save time, I order some steaks and sides and we have to make one last stop on the way home. I text Seb to double check he got my message earlier about picking up Moira's presents, 'cause if he didn't I need to drop her off and leave again, and I would much rather take her upstairs and fuck the shit out of her.

"Relax, I've got it handled," he assures me. "I'll be home shortly."

Sliding my phone back in my pocket, I help Moira take the bags inside the house, but before she can start unpacking everything, I grab her hand and drag her toward the stairs.

"What are you doing?" she protests, eyes widening. "I have to set up."

"I need to fuck you. It's medically necessary."

Biting back a grin, she says, "But... Sebastian's going to come home."

"Then he can join in. I don't care. I need to fuck you."

"Dammit, Griff," she says, but follows right behind me. "Can't you wait until later for your presents? You're worse than a kid on Christmas."

"Shouldn't have offered up such a good present," I tell her.

MOIRA

One minute I'm worried about the steaks that are getting cold, the table cloth that is certainly not being put on the table, the candles that are not being lit, and all the Valentine's Day festivity that is not being set up downstairs for Sebastian.

The next minute Griff is throwing me down on our bed and ripping my red skirt up. I gasp in surprise, then his rough hands rip my lacy panties off and spread my thighs apart. My stomach sinks with arousal as he gazes at me hotly, then buries his face between my legs and devours me like *I'm* his box of chocolates.

"Oh, God, Griff." My head falls back against the mattress, my hands digging into the bed sheets.

Between the unexpectedness, how turned on I got teasing him back at the lingerie shop, and his fervor, I don't last long. I'm used to coming hard and fast when Sebastian or Griff eats me out, but more often than not, the other is kissing me or stimulating my breasts, so my body doesn't stand a chance.

This time it's all Griff. His open hunger sets me on fire, sending waves of pleasure crashing through my body.

He eases back, but narrows his eyes at me as I lie here, boneless. "Don't you get too comfortable, baby. I'm not done with you yet."

"Oh, I hope not," I reply, lightly. Griff shoves his pants down in one smooth motion and climbs on the bed, moving over me. I can't resist reaching a hand up to tenderly caress his face. "Do I get *my* Valentine's Day present now?" I tease.

"You get whatever you want," he promises.

"Good," I say, tugging his face close, hovering just above his lips. "Because I want you."

I see the pleasure and affection in his eyes at my words, his appreciation for the haven of safety he never knew until I gave it to him.

But then, like a wall sliding in place, he shuts it off. Excitement courses through my veins because he looks mean. I've seen Griff turn mean mode on for me on only a few occasions.

It always means *very* good things for me.

I *am* going to get my present.

He reaches down and grabs a brutal fistful of hair, yanking my head to the side and bending to leave a rough trail of hot kisses down my neck. I shudder, my eyes drifting shut, every nerve ending on my body coming alive.

"More," I gasp.

He yanks my hair and answers, "Is that how you ask?"

I could die, I'm so happy. "Please. Please, Griff."

"That's better," he murmurs, rewarding me with a few sweet kisses along my jawline, then he switches lanes and claims my mouth in a hard, brutal kiss that leaves me gasping and groping, needing more of him, needing him inside me.

A new voice joins the fray, and my arousal soars to new heights. "Tell him how much you want it, sweetheart."

I pry my eyes open to look over at my gorgeous husband as he closes the bedroom door behind him, then deposits his coat on the chair in the corner.

Griff pulls away, glancing at my husband for direction. Should he keep going, or does Sebastian want to join in?

Sebastian waves a hand, granting his permission. "Go ahead; you seem to have things under control. I'll jump in when I'm ready."

Well, now that he's here, I want them both. I'm greedy. When I meet Griff's gaze, I see immediately that he understands. He releases his hold on my hair and leans down to do what he enjoys better anyway—the tender kisses, the soft caresses. Sebastian is here to play his role now, so Griff doesn't need to.

I'm only disappointed for a whisper of a second. There will be countless other opportunities to play with Griff alone. That's one of the many perks of all of us sharing our lives together.

Now that he's here, I reach a hand out to Sebastian, beckoning him closer to the bed. My beautiful husband doesn't need to be beckoned; he's already on his way.

As I lie here pinned beneath Griff's powerful body, his big hands roaming beneath my shirt, Sebastian leans down and gives me a lingering kiss. "Hello, sweetheart."

"Hi, honey. How was work?"

Griff laughs and Sebastian grins at him, then climbs on the bed and grasps his beautiful cock, drawing my eyes to that magnificent instrument. "Never as good as home."

"That's for damn sure," Griff agrees. "Nothing's better than home."

I glow, because that's mine. I do that. I'm the reason they both love home so much.

"You didn't even fully undress her," Sebastian says, upon noticing I'm still dressed in my red skirt and cream colored top.

"I was too fucking impatient," Griff explains. "She tormented me."

"You love when she torments you," Sebastian points out.

"I didn't say I didn't love it. I just needed to bury my cock in one of her holes and I didn't want to get arrested."

I cover my face with my hands, helplessly grinning. "You guys, I'm right here. You can't just talk about my holes when I'm right here."

Bringing his cock closer to my face, my husband tells me, "We can do whatever we want, sweetheart."

His words cause my pussy to clench, and me to feel his absence. I squeeze my legs together, squirming with need. I reach a hand up to grasp Sebastian's cock and pleasure courses through me when he briefly closes his eyes, enjoying my touch. My stomach twists up with need. I lift my head up off the bed and taste him, running my tongue along the underside of him. It's not enough. I need more. I need all of him. I grasp his shaft and guide it into my mouth, closing my lips around him and sucking on the head.

"Mm, good girl. Deeper."

I need to switch positions. I'm flexible, but I'm not a fucking rubber band. I pop off his dick and look up at Griff. "Can we move? I need to—"

Griff moves and I sit up, dragging my white top off and tossing it on the floor. Before I can get my bra off, Sebastian takes over, dragging my legs in his direction. "I'm going to take your pussy tonight. Griff can have your mouth."

I look up in time to see Griff shoot Sebastian a faint look of displeasure, but my husband isn't one to dawdle. Now that he's claimed his territory, he slides his long, elegant fingers inside me and I moan, pushing against his hand. I want to share the pleasure with Griff, so I open my mouth and lean forward, taking most of him into my mouth. Already I can feel the faint displeasure melting out of him; I can feel the pleasure I'm giving him take its place as I run my tongue along his hard length. I relax my throat and take the rest of him. I want to look up at his handsome face, I want to watch him fuck my mouth, but my husband—finding me already drenched and ready for him—positions his crown at my entrance and I know I won't have enough control of my own movements once he starts fucking me. Once they start going at me from both ends, I'm more or less at their mercy. It's the hottest thing ever.

Before invading me, Sebastian reaches forward and runs his fingers along my throat, caressing me even as I work Griff's cock. Sebastian's hand drops to my breasts. He palms one, then pushes his hand inside the delicate fabric and pinches my nipple. I gasp and he thrusts his hips forward, shoving inside me. I moan around Griff's cock. Sensing my need, Griff threads his big fingers into my hair, caressing me tenderly while I suck him.

"You're perfect, Moira," he tells me, rocking his hips forward, pushing deep into my throat. The pleasure in his voice is like an aphrodisiac in and of itself.

But I'm not perfect; they are. Griff is perfect with his tenderness, caressing and worshiping me in the most obvious way with his reverence. And my brutal, perfect husband worshiping me in the effortless way only he can, with his merciless thrusts, filthy words, and punishing yanks of my hair. As is always the case when they team up to take me, I'm driven mindless with pleasure, with the push and pull, the give and take, the pleasure they both get from my body. I get it back tenfold.

When he can tell his best friend is getting close, Sebastian sends waves of arousal crashing through me, commanding Griff, "Come down my wife's beautiful throat."

Now Griff's hand in my hair shifts from tender to possessive.

Sometimes he likes when Sebastian pokes at him, saying things like that. Other times he feels the need to remind Sebastian I'm his, too. Right now it seems to be enough to grab my hair more roughly, to shove himself more forcefully into my eager mouth. God, I love when Sebastian pisses him off. Only sexually, of course. It doesn't last. Griff doesn't want to be angry, so he lets it all out and I take everything he needs to give me—with pleasure.

Since Griff finished first, he caresses my face one more time and pulls out so Sebastian can finish. I look up coyly, licking my lips to get every last drop of him.

"Fuck, you're beautiful," he tells me.

"Your filthy little angel," I say, mischievously.

Chuckling lightly as he eases over onto his spot on the bed, he says, "Always."

Sebastian pulls out of me and rolls me on my back now that he's done sharing for the moment. Peace settles over me as my husband comes down fully on top of me. I love the weight of him crushing me, the feel of his skin against mine. I reach up and run my fingers through his dark hair, gazing at him with all the love in the world, yet it barely scratches the surface of what I feel for him. He leans closer and, for a couple seconds, rests his forehead against mine.

My pussy may be currently empty, but my heart is full. I love this man so much.

His energy shifts, the loving gentleness replaced with control. He gathers my hands at the wrist and shoves them over my head, pinning them with one hand, narrowing his intense blue eyes at me. My pulse kicks up several speeds, even though I know he isn't really angry with me. It never gets old playing with him.

"Should I punish you for how much you enjoyed Griff's cock, little wife?"

Oh yes.

It seems impossible, but I feel the area between my thighs get even damper.

And then my husband delivers on Griff's earlier promise to give me whatever I want. He stakes his claim and owns my body. When my pleasure reaches its peak and I come apart in his arms; he holds me close, then with a few final thrusts, joins me in paradise.

I love every part of having both of these big, strong men possessing me, but now might be my favorite. Griff moves closer now that we're all sated, draping an arm across my waist and snuggling me on the right. Seb stays close on my left side, settling his hand on my hip and nuzzling his face in my neck.

Sighing, I announce, "You gentlemen give the best gifts."

I feel Sebastian's breath against my skin as he chuckles, then drops a kiss on the ball of my shoulder. "We didn't give you your gifts yet."

"Pretty sure you did. Also pretty sure our steaks are cold and gross by now."

"I couldn't give less fucks about steak right now," Sebastian states.

"I wanted us to have a nice Valentine's dinner. This is our first Valentine's Day all together."

Griff caresses my stomach. "Trust me, baby, we enjoyed this more than steak."

"And I'm still expecting my annual gift," Sebastian adds.

"Oh, don't you worry. I bought lots of lingerie. Maybe when we do this again later, you gentlemen can take the time to fully undress me before you fuck me."

"We will," Sebastian assures me. "That was Griff's fault. He should've already had you naked when I came in."

"I was busy making her come on my face," Griff states.

Cocking an eyebrow and nodding in acknowledgement, Sebastian says, "That's a pretty good reason."

I sigh, regretfully pushing myself up. I could remain here cuddling with them all night long, but I want to feed them and execute our original plan for tonight, too. "I'm going to go put myself back together, then I'm going downstairs and setting up all my Valentine's day stuff. I want you to be surprised, so don't come down until I say you can."

SEBASTIAN

As my dutiful little wife cleans up, rights her clothing, and heads downstairs to decorate the house for us, I relax in bed sheets that still smell like her and consider how long this Valentine's night production will take before we can get her back here again. It's sweet that she likes to go all out for us, but I'm eager to get back to my favorite part of the evening.

As soon as she's gone, Griff glances over at me, keeping his voice low, like he's still worried she might hear. "Did you stop and pick up the bracelet?"

"Of course I did. I put it in your trunk along with the flowers. When we go downstairs, I'll keep her busy and you can run out and grab them."

Breathing a sigh of relief, he says, "Great, thank you."

"She wouldn't have minded waiting until tomorrow," I point out.

He shakes his head. "Years of conditioning. Ashley would've ripped my head off."

"Fuck Ashley," I mutter.

"We don't have to talk about Ashley," he says, a little more firmly. Then he glances my way again and steps on more neutral ground. "What'd you get her?"

"Diamond necklace, a box of biscotti dipped in Belgian chocolate, and chocolate covered strawberries for dessert tonight."

Smirking faintly, Griff says, "Or maybe for dinner. The steaks are probably cold now."

I shrug. "We've eaten worse than warmed up steak in our time."

"That's true," he allows.

"Overall, a better Valentine's Day than your last one?"

"Much better." Griff nods his head, looking like he's lost in a memory, but he doesn't offer any insight into what it might be. He used to talk to me about Ashley, but even though it's been nearly a year, he still hates bringing her up to me now. It bothered me a little at first, but it doesn't anymore. Regardless of how he feels about the situation, it doesn't get in our way, so I don't lose any sleep over it.

Since we've got some time to kill while we wait for Moira, we relax here, bullshitting and talking business. Then Griff tells me he wants to do something special for Moira since our first official anniversary is coming up. I tell him he's more than welcome to if he wants to plan it himself—I already have a wedding anniversary to keep track of; I don't need a second one.

Moira finally shoots me a text that we can come back downstairs. While Griff gets dressed in the bathroom, I pull my clothes on out here. I leave the tie off and my top few buttons undone since Moira isn't here to fiddle with it.

I stop outside the bathroom door and rap on it lightly with my knuckles. "I'm gonna go downstairs now. You can grab the stuff out of your car and meet us in the kitchen afterward."

"That works. Thanks again for picking it up for me."

24

"No problem."

When I get down to the kitchen, I get a lovely view—not the romantic décor she lovingly exploded all over the room, but my wife's ass bent over as she reaches into the oven and pulls out a pan that smells like brownies. She's not wearing the cream-colored blouse and red skirt she left the bedroom in, but a see-through lace contraption with a matching pink thong, and two tiny triangles of fabric over her breasts, tied together by little more than a string. Fuck, she is beautiful. I wait until she puts the pan of brownies down on the stovetop, then I come up behind her and encircle her waist with my arms.

"Happy Valentine's Day, gorgeous."

Moira leans back into me, securing her hands on my forearms. "Thank you, honey. Happy Valentine's Day to you, too. I should probably warn you; I got you a super sappy card."

"How sappy are we talking?"

"Wear gloves when you open it, otherwise you're gonna get pretty sticky."

I smile, nuzzling my face into the curve of her neck and leaving a few kisses. "If I'm gonna get sticky opening something, I'd much rather it be my present." Her head falls back against my shoulder as I drop one of my hands from around her waist and reach down to rub her between the legs.

A bit dazedly, she murmurs, "It's nice of you to keep accepting the same present year after year. You already own the damn thing, you know."

"I do know. It's the only present I ever want," I assure her, my lips moving to her jaw. "Besides, I like all the different ways you wrap it up."

Her lips tug up in a smile, but she keeps her eyes closed. "For the entire 65 seconds you let me keep it on."

"How's Griff enjoying *his* present?"

She sighs again, moving against me as I slide a finger inside her. "He enjoyed it quite a lot. You were right. He loved being the one I called to come rescue me."

Satisfied, I nod. "Good."

"Did you bring the car back home?"

I shake my head. "Didn't want him to get suspicious. I'll pick it up tomorrow after it's 'fixed.'"

Biting her bottom lip and moaning low in her throat, Moira brings her arm up to wind around my neck and draw me closer. She sighs with pleasure. "I love you, Sebastian."

Moira already knows exactly how much she means to me, but I'll never tire of telling her. Never tire of showing her. Right before I make her come, I kiss the shell of her ear and murmur, "I love you, too, sweetheart."

THE MORELLI FAMILY

BONUS DELETED SCENE

There already exists a deleted scenes collection for the Morelli family series (*Entrapment*, if you missed it), but there is one scene I decided not to include, and that scene has since been requested many times by many readers. So, I decided to write it. I know not everyone wants it, and that's fine. This scene is optional. I priced this ebook based only on the two short stories; I threw this one in for free. If you don't want to read it, skip straight ahead to the sweet treat, <u>A Perfect Valentine's Day!</u>

I've positioned it before the Valentine's Day story since this scene happens long before that one, and also because *A Perfect Valentine's Day* is the place I would like to leave you in at the end of this treat bundle, not this one. If you're going to read both, make sure you read this one first.

This deleted scene takes place during *Last Words*, at the end of part one after Rafe and Mateo's scene in the study. Consequently, this takes place many months before Rafe comes back for Easter and meets Laurel.

If you feel you need to skip this scene to protect any of your warm and fuzzies for certain characters/pairings, no problem—just don't read it and disregard its existence. :)

Obviously parts two and three of *Last Words* happened after part one, so you already know how it all ended up and that this did no damage. That this happened *was* referenced in part three a few times, but I think it may have escaped the notice of some readers. I know Mateo can be a touch too kinky for some of you, and that's totally fine—you don't have to read this if you know you won't enjoy it. Mia and Mateo love, want and need **only** one another, so this is not required reading to appreciate their story.

The title of this sexy scene is ***Mateo/Mia/Rafe*** and it is exactly what it sounds like.

For everyone who has been asking for this scene, enjoy! :)

If that sounds like nothing you want to read, feel free to skip to the completely safe Valentine's Day short story, and wait for Rafe's book to see what he's like during sexy time. ;) Given the uniqueness of this situation, this may not be the best indicator anyway.

2

MATEO/MIA/RAFE

MIA

I lie in bed trying like hell to sleep, but it's impossible. The tension won't leave my body. Replaying over and over in my mind is the visual of my husband—my incredible, untouchable husband—being marched across the room, his lip bloody, his arms held tightly behind his back. Alec's accusations traipse across my mind, leaving a trail of inky dread behind them. Dante's resentful words lance me.

Mateo is my heart and soul, and I put him in danger. It doesn't matter that it wasn't real. It doesn't matter if he was only performing for me.

It could have been real.

I bought so completely into Mateo's legend, his presence, his reputation, it just never occurred to me that by trying to help others, I could hurt him. Not really. Not until tonight.

Tonight I felt it. Tonight I felt a lot of things.

And right now what I feel is overwhelming anxiety that my husband hasn't come back to bed yet. I tell myself he's safe because there's no reason he wouldn't be—tonight was a production. Only a production.

Their words were real, though, and they are still running through my head. No matter how imaginary the events may have been, it was real to me as it was happening. The consequences felt *real*.

Another thing is, Rafe is still here, and I still don't completely trust him. I don't completely trust Dante, either. I trust Adrian with my life on a daily basis, but even he lied to me. If he was in the closet tonight to make sure things didn't go sideways, he *did* know what was going on. When I told him how worried Rafe was making me, he told me he didn't think Rafe's behavior toward me had anything to do with why he was in town, and that was bullshit.

Right now, in the aftermath of what just happened tonight, I don't feel like it's worth trusting anyone. I just want to curl up with Mateo and stay in our little bubble forever.

Thank god, my husband saved me from reality again tonight.

Now I need him to save me from my *memories* of tonight. When I was wrapped up in him, when our bodies were one and his strong arms held me, both of us safe and sound, it was over. The feelings lingered, but they were just an uncomfortable memory, not a real threat. He let me get lost in him, but now that he has been gone for so long, my worries are coming back.

I'll say one thing about my husband—he doesn't half-ass teaching a lesson. That man goes big and makes it stick.

After a few more anxious minutes, the door opens and a faint sigh of relief escapes me. He's back. Now he'll strip his clothes off, climb into our bed, pull me close, and absorb all my fear. He'll comfort me with his presence and banish every last shred of doubt. Mateo will be just fine—as long as I keep my ass out of his way.

I'll stay out of his way.

Peace and contentment flow through me as I hear him shut the door, as I hear the soft sounds of his shoes against the bedroom floor. Then I frown faintly. That sounds like more movement than I expected.

Fear slices through me, reminding me of earlier when Dante darkened our doorway. My heart pounds and I turn over, my gaze seeking out the shape of my husband.

I find him, but before I can feel too relieved, I see a second body. My eyes widen, my heart falls clear through my stomach, and I start to sit up. Remembering I'm naked, I wrap the soft white sheet around my body more carefully.

Mateo approaches my side of the bed, but his carriage is calm. There's no urgency, no hardness outside of the layer of exterior he always has up when other people are around.

"You awake?" His deep voice pours over me like honey and I smile up at him. His big hand comes toward my face and he runs his knuckles across my cheek, watching me with a tender glow in his dark eyes. God, I love this man.

I nod my head. "I was waiting for you to come back to bed."

"Here I am," he offers.

"Yes.... But I thought you'd be coming back alone. I'm kinda naked under here."

Amusement flickers in his dark gaze. "I remember."

"So, are you coming to bed soon?"

He drags his fingers across my jaw a little more deliberately. "Mm hmm."

A soft hint of discomfort tugs at me. "Why is he here?"

The other figure in the room has been lurking at the foot of the bed while we talked, like a shadow that wouldn't come to life until acknowledged. Now, Rafe Morelli takes several slow steps forward, his hooded gaze on me. It should be on my face—*only* my face—but like my husband, Rafe doesn't excel at respecting boundaries. Instead, his dark gaze traces the curve of my bare shoulder, the wrinkled line of the sheet I'm holding across my breasts like my life depends upon it. I don't like the way he's looking at me—like I'm not a married woman, like my husband isn't standing right here, like he's going to get a peek beneath this sheet, and he's damn sure of it.

My stomach flutters with nerves and my gaze flashes back to Mateo. He hasn't answered me, so I reword and ask, "Mateo, what's going on?"

"I need you to do something for me, sweetheart."

My heart beats faster in anticipation. I know that tone—deliberately calm, oozing authority. He's going to issue a command I'm not going to want to follow, and he's priming me to do it anyway. "What do you need me to do?" I ask, tentatively.

"You're going to help me pay a debt," Mateo states, his finger dropping from my face. He trails it lightly across my collar bone, prodding lightly at the sheet I'm still clutching close.

"A debt?" I ask, cautiously.

Now he hooks his finger on the inside of the sheet and tugs. I push my hand more firmly against my chest, but he has only to cock an eyebrow at me and my heart pounds, my grip easing. He drags the sheet away from my breasts and I take a shuddering breath. I'm tempted to look at Rafe, but I keep my gaze locked on my husband's. What the hell is he doing?

"Mm, very nice," Rafe murmurs, in approval.

"Aren't they?" Mateo remarks, casually.

I try to go along with whatever the hell Mateo wants from me, but I can't. I bring my hands up to cover my breasts, shooting a dirty look at Rafe, then at Mateo. "What the hell are you two doing?"

"Playing," Rafe offers, taking a seat on the edge of my bed.

34

I scoot back, putting more distance between us. "I'm not your toy."

Now a slow grin splits his face, somewhat predatory—but not the way he has been this past couple weeks, more like the way he was that first day I met him in Vegas. "Don't I know it, little one. Mateo found you first; otherwise I think we both know you would be."

I squirm, shaking my head stubbornly. "I don't know that."

"If you're going to lie, at least do it to someone who might believe you," Rafe advises.

"Your fibs are wasted on us, sweetheart."

I shoot my husband a dirty look. "You... What the hell, Mateo?"

"You two have some tension to work out," Mateo informs me. "Rafe got to play with you once and I didn't even get to watch."

Shame floods me and I have to look away. I can't believe he would bring that up at all, but in front of Rafe?

"There it is," Rafe says, like he's just found Waldo.

"Like I said," Mateo responds.

I don't like the feeling of them talking *about* me right in front of me. "I don't want Rafe in our bedroom. Please make him leave."

"No," Mateo says, simply.

My gaze jumps to him and my eyes widen. "No?"

He nods. "No."

"But..."

Mateo watches me for a moment, then says, "Rafe, give me a minute with my wife."

Relief pours through me. I only need a minute alone with him to talk him out of whatever stupid idea he has. When Rafe is around, I can't talk to Mateo as freely. As soon as the door clicks shut and Rafe is safely on the other side of it, I crawl forward, grabbing onto my handsome husband and drawing him close. Clearly he's lost his mind and he requires help to find it.

"What are you doing?" I ask, leaning my naked body against him. One of his hands moves to the small of my back and he gazes down at me, waiting to hear my objections. "This is insane. Rafe shouldn't be here. This is *our* bedroom. He shouldn't be in our space."

With a look more knowing that I'm comfortable with, Mateo caresses my jaw with his free hand and tells me, "He's already in it."

I get the feeling he doesn't mean because *he* invited him. Guilt multiplies inside me and a lump forms in my throat. "You said you forgave me. You've said it a million times."

"I'm not the problem, Mia," he says, gently. "I'm over it. You're not. Even my ordering you on multiple occasions hasn't worked to completely free you from the guilt. It comes back when he does. That's not getting over it. Time to try something else."

"Not this," I say desperately, shaking my head. "I'll do better. I'll let it go. I promise. I don't want anyone else, Mateo. I only want *you*—forever. I don't want Rafe, and I don't see how anything that could possibly come from Rafe being in our bedroom when I'm naked could make me feel *less* guilty."

"Because I'm in control of this," he says, simply. "This is my call. You're doing what I tell you to do, not acting of your own volition. This time, you get no say."

I sit back on my heels, looking up at him curiously. This is not the first time he's pulled rank and taken my consent out of the equation, but it is the craziest. "I get no say," I repeat.

Holding my gaze, he nods his head once. "You're doing this because *I* want you to. I want to watch you with him. I want both of us to play with you. Just for tonight. Then you can see that I mean it when I say it doesn't bother me."

I bite down on my bottom lip, still skeptical. I'm starting to see the logic in what he says—it takes the responsibility off my shoulders when Mateo makes me do things. He can't really make me do anything I don't want to do, because I *want* to do whatever pleases him. I get pleasure by giving it to him. If he's doing it for me, I don't want to do it, but he's telling me it's what *he* wants. If I could fully believe that, I could get on board, but there's a part of my brain that doesn't believe him.

Maybe the part that's been there.

God, I don't want to bring that up.

"You're talking about another threesome," I say.

Since he also knows we don't talk about that, his dark eyebrows rise slightly in surprise that I'm bringing it up. He recovers quickly, because he's Mateo, but then he nods. "Yes—this one should be more your speed, don't you think?"

How can he joke at a time like this? "I don't want to have a threesome with Rafe," I inform him. "Just like I didn't want to have a threesome with Meg."

"Yes, well, I can't get you Adrian," he remarks, his eyes flashing with mischief as he takes a seat on the edge of the bed.

I roll my eyes and crawl toward him again, lifting his arm around me and nestling into his side. I wrap my arms tightly around his torso and mutter, "I don't want a threesome with Adrian either. I told you, that's just a kinky story I tell to get *you* going."

If he believes me, you certainly can't tell. "Well, tonight, we can actually do it."

"But I don't want to."

"Stop saying that. I don't like when you lie to me."

I pull back and frown at him. "I'm not lying to you."

"I can feel the tension between you, Mia. Who do you think you're talking to?"

That makes me feel absolutely wretched. Before I can help it, tears well up in my eyes at the thought of him feeling like I want anyone else.

He sighs and wraps his arm back around me, pulling me close. "Don't look like that. I already told you, I'm not upset. I never want you to feel ashamed of your sexuality, Mia. It's one of my favorite things about you. Your attraction to Rafe happens to work in my favor in this instance. I'm not just doing this for you; there's a whole list of other reasons I've decided this is the right move. My sexually capable cousin helping me overload my little wife with orgasms seems like a good enough reason to make the list, though."

I squeeze him tight. "You give me lots of orgasms. All the orgasms I need. You just gave me two a couple hours ago."

"Yes, I am aware of all this," he says, dryly.

"So, make Rafe go back to his room, we can forget this ever happened, and *you* can give me all the orgasms you want."

"All right," he says, far too easily. "If you can tell me in explicit detail about the night he made you come in Vegas, I'll say fuck the rest of my reasons and I'll do that." Tugging me back, he watches expectantly, like he's my professor awaiting an oral exam.

I stare at him. He knows I can't—won't—do that.

"Go on," Mateo says. "I want every detail. I want to know how he tasted, how he felt against your skin—"

I shrug out of his hold and roll away. "Stop it, Mateo."

He stops talking, but he stands. "I'm going to get him. This is the quickest, easiest, and best solution to a host of my problems. This is the most important. I won't have shit like this between us, Mia. It's stupid. It's beneath us."

"You won't like it," I burst out, jumping off the bed to follow him. I grab his arm to stop him. "It's not fun. I don't know why you think it will be, but it isn't. It's stressful and awful and it makes your stomach hurt. And I didn't even have to watch—whatever I'm sure he'll want to do. We had strict rules, and I still hated every minute that you weren't just touching me, and I felt awkward when you *were* touching me, every minute that she was even in the room with us. Knowing it happened is not the same as seeing it, trust me."

It's annoying how patient he looks. "Mia, this is not the first time I've watched you with someone else. You and I are different people. I know you didn't enjoy that, that's why we never attempted it again. This is entirely different. I've *already* watched someone else fuck you—Vince, on a monitor." Now he grabs my arm and yanks me against him, running his fingers lightly down my shoulder. "I know you don't understand because it's just how you are, and it's all you know, but thinking of you with Rafe—in front of me—doesn't make me feel jealous. You're all mine—what do I have to be jealous of? Watching you is intoxicating. Your pleasure is beautiful. You're so responsive, so passionate. You *feel* so much. I love watching you. It doesn't make me feel the way it would make you feel. It turns me on."

"Just the thought of it makes me want to claw your skin off," I state.

He lips curve up and he rubs my back reassuringly. "You have before. Rest assured you can retract your claws; I'm never going to touch anyone else ever again."

I already know that, but now he wants *me* to touch someone else. "I just don't see how you can enjoy this."

"*You* will enjoy this," he murmurs, running his lips along the shell of my ear. "Two dangerous, powerful men using your body for their pleasure."

Despite my reluctance, I feel a twinge between my legs hearing him word it that way.

"Rafe shares many of your kinks and I'll let him play with you however he wants. I have one rule, that's it."

I feel like asking will give the appearance that I'm considering this, so I keep my mouth shut.

He nibbles on my ear, causing goosebumps to rise up along my neck and arms. "Don't you want to know my rule?"

Still, I say nothing.

Apparently seeing he hasn't hooked me yet, Mateo continues, "Among the *many* differences between this time and that one, this is something everyone wants. Rafe wants to fuck you, sweetheart. To be honest, I expected he would when he had the chance in Vegas. He wants it enough to come here and do my bidding for these past two weeks, potentially putting himself at risk when he goes back home." Pulling back and glancing down at me, his brown eyes warm, he adds, "Before you met him, Rafe wouldn't have dumped a glass of water on me if I caught on fire. He's here for you, not me."

Now I can't help speaking. "That seems like a bad thing from where I'm standing. Look what happened with Vince."

Mateo shakes his head, dismissing my concern. "Rafe isn't Vince. He likes you because you're his type and you're mine, because you're a beautiful toy on a shelf he can't reach. He'll be satisfied playing with you; he doesn't need to keep you. There is a chance he'll try to wrest control away from me tonight just to fuck with me for my past trespasses against him, but I'm not worried. I have complete faith in you. I know you won't give in to him. You're mine, Mia; nobody else can ever really have you. When he fails, he'll lose interest. Then we can put all this behind us. You won't have to feel guilty because you'll know I'm *honestly* not upset by what happened, and he can stop wondering what it would be like to fuck you because he'll already know. One night and we all clear the air. Plus, you know, the debt thing."

"You seriously promised him *this* for his help?" I question.

Mateo shrugs. "It's all he wanted. He already has money and clout; I don't have much bargaining power with him."

That just reminds me of when Rafe first brought me home to Mateo, after I came clean about what had happened in Vegas between us and Mateo joined Rafe in the wing chairs in his study. I remember vaguely wanting to lie down on the floor between them, in front of the roaring fire, and just soak up their powerful presences.

As long as they're playing nice and I don't have to worry about treachery, they really are quite beautiful together. Mateo and all his seductive darkness, Rafe with his golden good looks. The visual creeps into my mind of both of them having free rein over my body—Rafe's hands on me, Mateo's intense presence hovering over me, watching.

I swallow and look up at him, a bit cautiously. I know he doesn't need much to pounce on. "You would both have me at the same time, or you'd only watch?"

"A little bit of both. We'll definitely both have you at the same time."

"You don't think you're too much alike? I'm not sure this works. When I imagine it with Adrian, that's different because Adrian is ultimately within your control. Rafe...."

"He's within yours," Mateo says, simply. "He might push your consent, but he won't take it. He's not like me."

Smiling faintly, I loop my arms around his neck and lean in to kiss him. "No one is like you."

"He'll try to tempt you, but he won't force you. At the end of the day, he knows he's a guest here. The games may be big league, I can't say for sure; I've never done this with him before. If I were him, I'd try, so be ready for it."

"Of course you would," I mutter. "What's the rule?"

41

A slow smile claims Mateo's lips and I realize I just said the magical words.

"I meant, *if* we——"

He doesn't let me finish backtracking. "The rule is simple. Play however you want, but don't kiss him on the mouth."

The addition of "on the mouth" fills my mind with naughty images—Rafe standing above me, me kneeling on the ground in front of him. "I can kiss him... in other places," I say, to reiterate.

"Yes, of course," Mateo says, easily. "I want you to enjoy yourself. I don't want this to be a stressful experience for you. There's one simple rule, and that's it. He already knows the rule—well, he has two, but he can handle two."

"What's his other rule?" I ask, out of curiosity.

"When he's inside you, he has to wear a condom."

I bury my face in my hands, feeling heat beneath my skin at Mateo's words. "Another man shouldn't be inside me at all."

He grabs my wrist, tugging my hands away from my face. "Nope, don't fall back; we're making good progress here."

I let him pull my hands away from my face and tug me back against him. Meeting his gaze, I ask seriously, "You're *positive* you want to do this?"

"Yep."

Yep, he says. Like it's so freaking simple. God, he's a peculiar man. I love the hell out of him, but I swear, he's going to drive me out of my mind. "Tell me the other reasons."

"Hm?"

"The other reasons. You said you have a list."

Instantly dismissing my request, he tells me, "Don't concern yourself with my reasons. Know that I have a more than a half dozen *aside* from your pleasure, so it's a considered decision."

"There are *that many* reasons to do this? And you can't tell me any of them? Are they mean? Is this a trick? A test?"

"Stop asking so many questions and obey your husband," he tells me.

I give him a puppy dog pout. "Just one reason? A nice one? Please?"

Mateo rolls his eyes at me, but indulges me anyway. "Fine. Since he can't take control from me, he won't attempt to steal you away, but because of tonight, he *will* still be invested in protecting you. The experience will bond him to you in a way nothing else would. Vegas already bonded him enough to make this past couple weeks happen, and he didn't even get an orgasm out of that; tonight will seal the deal. Should anything ever happen to me, Adrian would obviously protect you, but if anything happens to me, there's a good chance he goes down, too. If something happens to me, Rafe will find out. He'll know you're vulnerable. Instead of leaving you to fend for yourself, he'll extract you and bring you to safety because he'll care about your well-being."

I make a face, my stomach sinking at the idea of there ever being a time where that might happen. "*That's* the nice reason?"

"The nicest one I have to offer," he verifies.

"Ugh, then don't tell me any of the other ones."

Mateo smirks, reaching down and tucking a chunk of hair behind my ears. "I didn't plan to."

"I don't like talking about you dying. You have to live forever. We already talked about this."

"Even in that case, Rafe caring about you has already proven beneficial to me. He'll do things for me now he never would have before he met you. Who knows all the ways this could potentially benefit me?"

The way this man's mind works, I swear. "You're so devious."

"Yes," he agrees.

I shake my head at him. "You're lucky I love you."

Dragging my hand to his mouth, he kisses my knuckles, then

flattens it against his heart and tells me, "I am well aware of my good fortune."

Now that he's won the argument, Mateo tells me to get back on the bed and he goes to the door to get Rafe. I'm still not sure this is a good idea, so I climb under the covers and pull the sheets up to cover my breasts again. I'm not entirely sure what my strategy is here, but the prospect of tonight seems daunting and I don't want to be on display as soon as he comes in.

"Are we good in here?" Rafe asks, looking at Mateo, then me.

"We are," Mateo says.

Rafe waits for me to answer, but I just look down at the sheets and fidget.

Crossing the room, Rafe takes a seat on the edge of my bed again. "Little one?"

I look to Mateo for guidance, but Rafe knows exactly what I'm doing and cuts me off before I can get anything. Gently grasping my jaw, he turns my face to look at him instead.

"I'm talking to you, not him," Rafe states, firmly.

My heart kicks up a few speeds. I already feel like he's disregarding Mateo and he hasn't even taken any clothing off. Mateo is wrong about this, I can feel it. I don't know what his other reasons are, but this is a bad idea.

"Mia," Rafe says, more sharply.

My gaze jerks to his. "Yes."

His gaze warms. A faintly sensual smile tugs at his lips and his grip on my jaw turns into a caress. "Good."

Fuck, did I just agree to this? I think I did. It wasn't exactly my intention, but then he snapped and I just... I didn't want to disappoint him.

This is a bad idea.

"I'm nervous," I blurt.

He nods, maintaining my gaze. "Why are you nervous?"

"I'm not sure you two are compatible in this way," I say carefully.

Rafe smirks. "Well, we're not fucking each other, little one —just you."

"I know, that's what I meant, though. You're both too controlling."

"You love controlling," Rafe states.

"You're both used to being the alpha male in this scenario, and there can't be two. The law of nature dictates this does not end well. I don't want you to piss each other off, and I feel like it's inevitable in this situation."

Shaking his head, Rafe slides closer. I hold the sheet a little tighter, but he makes no move to take it away from me. Instead, he takes my hand, places it palm up on his lap and lightly runs his blunt fingertips across the delicate skin of my wrist.

Pleasure swallows me up instantaneously. My heart feels light, my stomach rocky, but in the nicest way. Some of my senses weaken, as if to make up for the sense of touch requiring every single bit of my focus. Mateo has done this to me before, usually only when we're fighting. It's such a simple, seemingly innocent thing to do, but something about it bowls over my defenses like they're nothing. All I can focus on is how nice it feels, how nice he is for making me feel that way. He traces the outside edge of my palm, then drags it toward my thumb. My eyes drift shut as he continues to touch me with just that one finger; my teeth come down on my bottom lip. I'm lost to feeling, and there's really nothing sexual happening yet.

What were we talking about? I can't remember. Did he ask me a question?

Now he rotates my hand palm down and uses his finger to trace a path along the slightly less sensitive topside of my hand. It still feels lovely, but now I'm more cognizant—or I try to be. My brain tries to resist the shut-off technique that shouldn't work, because it's so damn simple. I recall just a moment ago when Mateo's lips were brushing the skin where Rafe is running his fingers.

Only before I can feel guilty, I look up and see Mateo standing beside the bed. My pulse picks up and I watch him slowly unbutton his shirt while Rafe's finger makes its way up my arm to my shoulder. My skin prickles pleasantly and in the smoothest motion imaginable, Rafe is suddenly on his knees behind me, his strong hands kneading the tense muscles in my neck and shoulders.

Okay, so far, this is not, in fact, a bad idea. Everything that's happening right now resides firmly inside the city limits of Good-Idea-Ville.

Pleasure rolls through me in gentle waves as I watch my husband undress. God, I love watching that man undress. Getting an incredible neck message in the meantime makes the glorious experience even better.

Stripping his shirt off, Mateo reveals the familiar, toned torso that I curl up against every night. I search his face for some sign that he doesn't like seeing Rafe's hands on me, but I find only molten heat in my husband's eyes. My head lolls to the side as Rafe's fingers knead a particularly tense spot and I murmur, "You're good at that."

A low chuckle in my ear causes me to tense up all over again. Still kneading the muscles in my neck and shoulders, Rafe places a soft kiss against my shoulder blade. "I'm good at a lot of things, little one."

Oh, God, bad idea, bad idea!

"Relax," he commands, giving my shoulders a firm squeeze.

I swallow, watching as Mateo climbs on the bed and prowls toward me, his intense dark eyes locked on mine. My favorite predator. I reach my arms out to him, needing him to come closer and reassure me.

Only *I* ask the big, bad wolf for reassurance.

Because I do, he gives it to me. Uncaring of Rafe's hands messaging me, Mateo rips the sheet away and drags me closer. I can't kiss Rafe, but I can certainly kiss him. Mateo claims my mouth in a hard, reassuring kiss so powerful it has me leaning away from Rafe's magical hands.

Rafe releases me and I go to my husband, abandoning the sheet to crawl forward. There's little point clinging to modesty when I know Rafe will see my body anyway. I brace my hands on Mateo's strong shoulders and close my eyes while he plunders my mouth. His hand creeps between my legs and I spread them obediently, waiting for his finger to move inside me. It doesn't. He runs a hand down my thigh and I moan into the kiss. He pushes on my thigh, signaling me to spread them wider so I do.

Mateo breaks the kiss and pushes his fingers through my hair, grabbing a fistful with one hand. I don't know where he's leading me, but I go without question. He looks behind me for a few seconds, watching Rafe, I guess. Then he claims my lips again, and as he does, I'm startled by the sudden movement of Rafe's handsome face moving beneath my body.

Oh, god. I break the kiss to say something, to stop him, but then Rafe's beautiful mouth fastens onto my pussy and I can scarcely breathe. Blood surges through my veins, then rushes to my head. He uses his tongue to explore the unfamiliar territory, but it's like he has a map. I shudder as his tongue touches every sensitive, hidden place. By instinct alone, I reach down and grab his hair. He growls into my pussy and does something incredible that draws a near-sob out of me.

Fuck. I open my mouth to say stop and Mateo must sense it, because he cuts me off, sealing his lips over mine. His kiss heightens my arousal to an unbearable degree. I already can't concentrate with Rafe's masterful tongue ravaging my pussy. I'm too overwhelmed by both of them, so I pull back from Mateo.

I need to focus on Rafe right now. It isn't a conscious decision; my brain is no longer invited to this party, robbed of its invitation by Rafe's sinful mouth. It's hard to breathe with him latched onto my pussy like this and I need to come so he'll let me go. I look down now and realize his fingers are digging into my thighs. A thrill shoots through me. He liked when I grabbed his hair, so I do it again, tugging it and bucking my hips against his face.

He offers up an approving chuckle, moving his hands to my ass and pulling me even tighter against his face.

"Oh, fucking fuck," I murmur mindlessly, raking my hands through my own hair.

He stops tasting my pussy just long enough to tell me, "Say my name, Mia."

"Rafe," I say, quietly at first. He uses his fingers to spread me and stabs his tongue inside me again, easily finding the path to pleasure he found before. He wraps his hands around my thighs again, digging his fingers into my soft skin. "Rafe," I cry again, a little less composed as his tongue sweeps inside me, wreaking havoc on my body's basic ability to function. In a disconnected way, I know I had concerns a minute ago, but damned if I can remember what any of them were. All I can think about is the tightening in my stomach, my heart slamming around in my chest as Rafe devours my pussy, as his fingers dig into my thighs like they belong to him, as I cry out his name and ride his face.

When his tongue takes me over the edge, I scream for him. His fingers dig in and I whimper his name. Shame sneaks in with the overload of satisfaction, but as pleasure explodes in my body, I can't focus on it. My orgasm is so intense—perhaps in part because it feels so wrong to come for Rafe—it drains the energy

48

out of my body. I'm putty in his hands as he snakes his arms up behind me and easily shifts my weight, rolling me onto my back and climbing on top of me.

I need him close, so I wrap my arms around him and pull him against me. I have a tenuous grip on anything outside of this moment, but I remember it's important that I don't kiss him on the mouth.

He gives me a cute little smirk and says, "That good, huh?"

I shove at his shoulder with all the strength of a limp noodle. "You know how good it was," I mutter.

Since it's all I can do, I bury my face in his shoulder. Then I kiss his neck, since I can't kiss his mouth. I wish I could. His mouth really deserves a thank you for that performance. My stomach still doesn't feel right. Fuck, I'm already tired. It doesn't help that this comes right on the heels of Mateo fucking me before he left earlier.

Since Rafe has me lying here, boneless and lacking the ability to resist, let alone the interest, he takes advantage. His big hand comes up to palm my breast. My nipple instantly pebbles for him, and the throbbing starts up again between my legs.

"Too bad we aren't at my house," Rafe murmurs, rolling my nipple between his thumb and forefinger. "I could break out a couple toys. You'd like playing with me, wouldn't you?"

"Yes," I whisper, closing my eyes.

His voice is so calmly commanding, so entrancing. I don't even have to pay attention as he lulls me with it. "Yes, of course you would. You'd let me do whatever I want to you, wouldn't you?"

"Yes."

His golden head drops and he takes my nipple into his mouth, brushing the other with his thumb to keep them both stimulated. I squirm already, my spent body somehow finding it within to need again. I can feel arousal gathering between my legs. Rafe's hand moves downward like he can hear my thoughts. It moves gently over my slightly swollen abdomen, then dips between my legs. I don't know what I want, exactly, but I let my legs fall open so he can have whatever it is he wants from me.

Rafe smiles at me approvingly.

"Fuck, look at this pretty little cunt."

I think he's talking to me, and then for a horrifying moment, I realize he's talking to Mateo. I try to squeeze my legs shut, but Rafe's hand holds one thigh in place and Mateo's shoots out to grab the other one, keeping me spread open for them to look at.

"Looks like she's enjoying herself," Mateo remarks.

"You love to be fucked, don't you, little one?"

My face flushes, but I don't answer. I would have a minute ago, but I can't get a good read on Mateo right now.

Rafe sinks a finger inside me while Mateo watches my face, hears the way my breath hitches. I meet his gaze, afraid for a moment, needing to know this is okay. It's too late if it isn't—he just watched me come so hard on Rafe's face that I legitimately forgot where I was for a minute, but he's poker facing me and I can't tell.

It breaks through the lust fog. The idea that maybe Mateo isn't okay with this.

"Stop," I tell Rafe.

Rafe doesn't stop. He keeps touching me, but after a moment, he frowns and looks at Mateo. "What's her safe word?"

Mateo doesn't take his eyes off me, and he still doesn't show me a sliver of emotion. "She doesn't have one."

Rafe's eyebrows shoot up and he withdraws his finger from my body. "She doesn't have a safe word? I'm not comfortable with that."

"I don't care," Mateo returns, levelly.

A knot of fear slides through my torso and I roll on my side, just so I'm not splayed here on my back anymore. I liked being on my back for them when I thought this was going okay, but now I'm not sure.

"Mateo?" I ask, quietly.

"Having fun?" His voice is cold, and it nearly stops my heart.

Alarm courses through me and I push up, stumbling on my not-quite recovered arms to sit up in front of him. "Are you okay?"

Instead of answering, he grabs my hair and shoves my face into the mattress, hard. Fear shoots through me, but I don't know if this is a game or it isn't. I have no idea. My hand shoots out and grasps whatever it can—his thigh. I swallow and try to lift my head up, but he pushes me back down.

Rafe has fallen silent, but I don't care. I only care that Mateo doesn't hate me. I care that I haven't hurt him. I care about making it up to him that he just watched me come for someone else. I knew he wouldn't be okay with it. I knew he was wrong.

I don't know if it will work this time, but I whisper, "Please. I need you."

The pressure on my head eases up. He lets me lift my head, then allows me to move closer and lean between his legs. He's hard as a rock and I want to relieve him, so I grasp his thick cock in my hand and rub, stealing a tentative look up at his face.

Still nothing. I wouldn't even know from his facial expression that I'm stroking him.

The fear intensifies. I drop my face between his legs and take his cock into my mouth, worshipping it with my lips and my hands, caressing him with my tongue. The taste of him drives me wild. Even with all the fear and uncertainty coursing through me, I can feel arousal drip between my legs as I suck the smooth head of his cock. I take him all next, clear into my throat. I care nothing for my comfort right now, only his. When he's lodged at the base of my throat, when he's completely invading me, I feel relief. I'll stay here all night if he lets me, sucking him, bringing him plea-sure, letting him know how sorry I am.

I hate disappointing him, but there's little as intoxicating as trying to make it up to him. My heart beats in my stomach, my nerves are a wreck, my pussy clenches around nothing, needing him to come inside, and all I can taste is my husband. All I can feel is his pull and his darkness. All I want is to feel his love, but he won't open that door yet. I need to convince him. I need to earn it. I moan around his perfect cock as I ease back and take him all again.

"Jesus, she is enthusiastic."

Rafe.

Cold fear shoots through me at the reminder and I suck harder. I rub my tongue along Mateo's length the way I know he loves. I moan again so he can feel my pleasure.

"Enough," Mateo says, sharply, tugging my hair.

Reluctantly, I pull my mouth off his cock and look up at him. I stay low because I feel low, because I need him above me. He still looks at me coldly and it shouldn't, but it turns me on more. I need to try harder. I need to do more.

"Please, Mateo."

His voice is hard. "Please what?"

"I need you inside me. Please."

"You need *me* inside you? You need me inside that pussy that's so wet for Rafe?"

My heart drops. The whole world ceases to rotate and I struggle to draw in a breath.

Then he grabs a fistful of hair, yanks me back on the bed, and moves over me, planting himself between my legs. I'm a little breathless, looking up at him with wide eyes.

He drops the poker face and smiles, familiar warmth coming back into those brown eyes as he murmurs, "Good."

My heart kicks forward and my whole body weakens with relief. I wrap my arms around my devious husband and pull him close, still not completely trusting it. "We're okay? Everything's good? You promise?"

Mateo answers my question by crushing his lips against mine in a kiss so possessive, my lips feel faintly bruised. He's not normally like this, and the sheer thrill of it intoxicates me. My desire for this man comes to life and beats between my legs. His tongue demands entrance between my lips and I open for him immediately, wrapping my legs around his hips and drawing him tightly against me. When he finally pulls back, he answers the invitation my hips are issuing. "We're not going to fill you up just yet, sweetheart."

Sweetheart. The endearment rolls over me like a salve.

Despite the convincing heat of his kiss, I need verification he isn't mad, so I run my hands over his pecs and meet his gaze. "You promise you're not mad at me?"

His hand comes up to caress my jaw, to cradle my face and pull me into him. "I promise."

I breathe a sigh of relief and burrow into Mateo's chest for comfort. He wraps his arms around me, one hand rubbing my back for reassurance. I'm craving his pleasure hard, so I reach between his legs to stroke him while he holds me.

"You two are something else," Rafe states.

Even though he only murmurs, Mateo sounds pretty self-satisfied. "Mm hmm."

"I've met some kinky bitches in my time, but none that have enjoyed having their *mind* quite so thoroughly fucked as part of a sexual experience. Isn't it sore from earlier tonight? It's like you've trained her to greet mental torture with insatiable lust."

"You wanna keep working up your diagnosis, or you wanna fuck my wife?" Mateo asks.

"That should be an easier decision," Rafe mutters, but I can still feel the bed move as he crawls closer. "I want to play with her first, but I want a safe word. She needs to know there's a way out if she wants one."

"No safe words," Mateo says, shaking his head. "We don't play that way."

"It isn't for you, it's for me."

"You're not giving my wife a safe word," he states, implacably.

Rafe's tone is hard and annoyed. "I *have* to."

Mateo answers back, slightly mocking. "Why? Is there an invisible judge here, making sure you adhere to your stupid rules? Will you be kicked out of the club if you break them once?"

"It's the only way I can know I'm not hurting her," Rafe states.

Unmoved, Mateo says, "I said no. Fuck her or don't, but none of that shit."

"You said I could play with her however I wanted to."

"You can."

"Why do you have to be such a fucking dick?"

Sensing the tension between them ratcheting up, I pull out of Mateo's embrace and turn toward Rafe. He's scowling at Mateo and the clash I was worried about seems inevitable, so I do my part to ease it.

Rafe's dark gaze shifts to me as I reach for his dress shirt and start undoing the buttons. Since I can still feel the agitation in his tense, muscled body, as soon as a swatch of tanned skin is exposed, I lean forward and kiss it. His gaze is still thunderous when I peer up at him, but as I slip the next few buttons through their holes and my kisses move lower and lower down his muscled torso, his annoyance begins to fade.

As many men as my husband pisses off, it's nice that this time he's pissing off one I can soothe with my body. I used to manage Vince that way on Sunday nights, but he was such a loose cannon.

He couldn't let it go. Rafe will probably let it go once I show him we can have fun and still play by Mateo's rules.

Now his shirt is undone, hanging open, and I peer up at him with a little smile as my fingers pull the buckle of his belt loose. I can feel how hard he is already beneath the fabric as my hand brushes him. He knows I followed up with kisses, so he must know where this is heading.

Judging by his hooded gaze as I draw off his belt, he does. He takes the strip of leather from me, fisting it in his strong hand, but then he seems to reconsider and tosses it off the side of the bed.

"Have you ever fucked another man's wife?" Mateo asks, almost conversationally.

"Not in front of him," Rafe replies dryly, keeping his eyes on me.

I drag down the zipper and push the button through his slacks, peering up at Rafe one more time before pulling them down past his hips. "Have you imagined this before?" I ask him.

"Of course I have," he replies.

Rubbing him through the fabric of his boxer briefs, I ask, "When was the first time?"

"When you made me breakfast. Should've just killed Vince and taken you that day."

His casual violence does things to me, even if I would never have wanted him to kill Vince.

"Fuck, I wish you *had*," Mateo mutters. "I would've completely forgiven you fucking my wife if I got a dead Vince out of it."

Rafe's lips curve up in faint amusement. "Why do you assume I would've given her back?"

That's not nice. I promptly drag down his underwear so I can turn his thoughts to much less antagonistic places, but not before Mateo replies easily, "Because I would've killed you if you hadn't."

"Guys, come on," I mutter. "Channel that violent energy into fucking me, not fucking with each other."

Mateo knee-crawls up behind me. His hand moves down the center of my back, then he smoothes it over my ass. "Suck Rafe's cock, sweetheart. I'm going to play with you while you do."

Oh, fuck.

Given not only permission, but instruction, I look over the impressive length and girth of Rafe Morelli. I'm used to a well-hung man, but I'm not disappointed to find tonight I get two of them. The closest I ever got to Rafe's cock in Vegas was in the pool. I felt his hardness between my legs, but he had swim shorts on, and I had bikini bottoms. He may have pushed his fingers inside, but never his cock.

"Like what you see?" Rafe asks.

"Why don't I show you?" I offer back, rather innocently considering the next thing I do is bend and take it into my mouth. Mateo shoves a finger into my pussy as I do, and I can't help moaning.

"Fuck," Rafe murmurs, brushing my hair off my neck and gathering it in his fist. "Just like that, little one."

I move my mouth over him slowly, dragging my tongue along the underside of his length as I go. I don't take him deep just yet; I want to play in the shallow end. I want to taste him the way he tasted me. With that in mind, I grip the base of him with my hand and run a flat tongue around his head like I'm licking an ice cream cone.

The sound of his low, gravelly tone above me brings me pleasure. "Christ, Mia."

Mateo shoves a second finger inside me and I moan again. I suck him hard, then soft. Mateo's fingers stoke my pleasure while I stoke Rafe's. Tension builds in my core as Mateo's expert fingers hit all the right spots with exactly the pressure he knows I need. The closer I get to coming for him, the more enthusiastic I am in my attention to Rafe's cock.

Then my husband's commanding voice rings out, obliterating even my own body's intentions. "Come for me, Mia."

He pumps his fingers into me as pleasure explodes inside me and I clench around them. I have only Rafe to hold onto, so I do, holding him close and moaning in helpless rapture, still with his cock in my mouth.

I'm too weak to continue when I come down. I pull off Rafe and sink into the mattress, needing a moment to rest and recover.

I don't really get one, because Mateo.

He lies next to me and slides an arm beneath me, pulling me against his hard body. I sigh with contentment and curl up with him, absently kissing his chest to express my gratitude.

"I love you," I murmur against his skin.

His voice is full of tenderness. "I know."

I smile and poke him, so he chuckles and kisses me on the forehead.

Now he addresses Rafe. "We're one and one. You want a turn, or should I take the next one?"

Next one? I start to ask what he's talking about, but then Rafe grabs my legs and drags me off my husband and halfway down the bed. I raise startled eyes to him and see he has shed the rest of his clothing, and now he's bare-ass naked, his cock ready and waiting for me. My heart drops as he says, "Mine."

Alarm courses through me. "I am not yours."

His lips curve up faintly. "I was talking to your husband, little one. I was claiming your next orgasm, not you."

Claiming my—?

One-and-one suddenly clicks into place. "Oh, my god, are you two seriously making orgasms competitive? Can't we all just enjoy this? Must there be a winner?"

"If that's the game, sounds like you're the clear winner," Mateo offers, his tone dry.

"Maybe we'll tie," Rafe offers, like that might make me feel better.

"You're impossible, ridiculous men," I inform them both.

"Well, we're the impossible, ridiculous men who are going to fuck you until you can't handle even one more orgasm," Rafe informs me, gathering my hands at the wrist and pushing them above my head. "So, it could be worse."

The man has an excellent point. I swallow, looking up at him. It's strange to have a man who isn't Mateo hovering above me in bed like this, but since he was here just a few hours ago, it also feels somewhat familiar. His beautiful, golden eyes are warm as he looks down at me, admiring the positioning of my body, raking over my breasts. My eyes drift to his shoulders—broad, strong shoulders, just the way I like them. I sigh a little, wanting to touch them, but he's still holding my hands above me right now. Flashes of the pool in Vegas drift back to me, how I rested my hands on his shoulders then. How he told me to spread my legs, and I did. How he touched me and commanded me to come for him.

Shame always follows quickly on the heels of those memories, so I usually don't let myself think about it. Mateo doesn't want me to feel badly about what he views as what I had to do to get back to him, but that's impossible. I love Mateo so much, and he's known so much hurt in his time. I want to be the one person who would never hurt him, and Rafe Morelli is the one tarnished spot on my record.

"Would you have helped me anyway?"

Rafe cocks an eyebrow. "What?"

"The night in the pool. In Vegas. If I hadn't let you touch me, would you have still helped me?"

Flicking a cautious glance Mateo's way, Rafe asks, "You really want to talk about that *now*, little one?"

"Yes," I reply. "I need to know. Mateo and I have different views of that night and I need to know who is right."

Now Mateo joins in with similar reluctance. "Mia... this is a palette cleanser, not a review of the facts. You don't need—"

I interrupt, "I *do*, Mateo." Looking back up at Rafe, my heart galloping in my chest, I say, "Can you just answer me, please?"

"Would I have helped you if I got nothing out of it?" he asks, nodding once, for clarification. "That's your question?"

I'm not sure that's exactly how I would word it—I could have offered him *something*, just nothing involving my body. That thought brings back Mateo's words earlier this night, and Rafe's words when I offered him anything Mateo could get him if he'd help me that first day in Vegas. Even Mateo admitted *he* doesn't have much bargaining power with Rafe—even my husband, whose supply of power feels endless to me most of the time, had to use *me* as his incentive to get Rafe's help.

Powerful men are harder to control; Mateo himself is evidence of that truth. There's no controlling the force of nature I married, and if Rafe has similar wealth and power, the same is probably true of him.

"No," Rafe answers simply. "Of course I wouldn't have helped you. You were a complete stranger to me. Do I look like the Red Cross? Why would I have helped you?"

I would have helped just because... well, when someone has been kidnapped, that's what you do. That's probably why I don't run a criminal organization and he does.

"I intended on taking much more than I did, little one. When I implied I might help if I got something out of it, I didn't mean fingering you in the swimming pool. We're not adolescents. I planned to fuck you—the same way this bastard fucked my ex-girlfriend. Even the score, even if it didn't matter anymore. Why not? The opportunity was there. Vince interrupted though, so I didn't get to issue my demands."

I swallow, my mind drifting back to Vegas. If his price to help me was sex, he sure didn't get it. "But you didn't fuck me. And you still helped. What changed your mind?"

Rafe watches my face for a moment, then he says, "You were softer and more open than I expected of someone who'd spent four years with Mateo. He tends to defeat people, cause them to shut down and retreat behind protective walls if not outright try to flee him, but you were wide open. And you were so sad. You missed this bastard so much." Finally, he shrugs. "At the end of the day, I wanted to ease your pain more than I wanted to stick it to him. Fucking you would have pissed him off, but that would have made you sadder." He releases my wrists and tenderly runs the back of his index finger along my jaw. "I didn't want to make you sadder."

My heart swells up with tenderness, but there's too much of it. It overflows and pours out so I'm floating along in an ocean of affection. I'm accustomed to that feeling, but only for Mateo. Vince never made me feel that way. Since my hands are free, I reach up to caress his strong jaw. "You're a good man, Rafe Morelli."

His warm brown eyes on mine, he smiles. "I'm really not."

"We can agree to disagree," I offer.

"Your whole mind needs recalibrating. Years with this guy have fucked up your scales."

The sound of Mateo's voice attracts my attention, especially because he sounds annoyed. "All right, are you going to spend the whole night chatting like schoolgirls at a slumber party, or are you planning to fuck her at some point?"

Instead of taking his bait, Rafe smirks. "He doesn't like us liking each other. Remember when you said you wouldn't get jealous, asshole?"

"I am not jealous," Mateo states carefully, like he's been insulted.

Rafe shakes his head at me, ignoring Mateo. "Fucking rookie, getting all jealous and shit."

I smother a smile, tipping my head back to regard Mateo. "You okay over there, baby?"

"Just bored," he offers, dryly. "I'm sure you can relate."

Rafe rolls his eyes. "Yeah, she's real bored." He sinks a finger inside me and I gasp at the unexpected intrusion. Drawing his finger out, he holds it up to show Mateo how wet I am, then shoves his finger into my mouth, still watching Mateo, and tells me, "Suck."

My face heats up, but I follow his order, sucking on his finger the same way I sucked on his cock.

"Does it taste like you're bored, little one?" Rafe asks.

I can't find my voice to contradict Mateo, but I shake my head wordlessly.

He must be done sparring with Mateo for the moment, because instead of poking at him anymore, Rafe shifts his weight, grabbing my thighs and lifting my body as he moves into the space between my thighs. I swallow down my nerves, watching as he guides his long cock until the head I sucked on is butting right up against my entrance.

"Condom," Mateo barks.

"She's already pregnant," Rafe points out. "If ever there was a time to skip the condom, this is it."

"And you've fucked every whore in Vegas. If you plan to finish all in one piece, you'll put a condom on first," Mateo advises.

Rafe scowls. "I do not fuck those girls without a condom."

"If you have a problem with my rules, we can stop."

"Yeah, you'd like that, wouldn't you?" Rafe taunts, but he drops my legs anyway and moves off the bed to retrieve a condom.

I look up at Mateo. That's the second time in the space of a couple minutes Rafe has said something along those lines, and Rafe is known for being especially observant. Does Mateo want to call a stop to this, but maybe his pride is getting in the way?

I reach an arm up toward him since Rafe isn't on the bed right now and Mateo climbs forward, hovering next to me. "Everything okay?" he asks.

"Are you sure you want to do this?" I ask, quietly. "He'll stop if I tell him to."

Mateo offers a faint smile, brushing his fingers through my hair. "I already told you—"

"I know what you told me, but it's okay to change your mind. This isn't the same as watching me with Vince, is it?"

"No, it's not," he admits.

I swallow, nodding my head. "So, we can just... stop. I can give him a hand job or go down on him to finish him off if you don't want to leave him hanging. He doesn't have to be inside me. We can skip this part." I reach my hand out to caress his face now. "I don't want you to experience any bad feelings over this. I'd rather stop."

Rafe is back on the bed now, condom in hand, but he sees me trying to bail, so he waits.

Mateo sits back, pulling away from the comfort I want to offer him. On second thought, he leans back down and gives me a lingering kiss on the mouth, then moves back to his spot to watch. "Proceed."

"Are you sure?" I ask, one more time.

"I'm positive."

Rafe slides the condom over his dick, not bothering to bait Mateo anymore. I think he knows how close I am to bailing, regardless of what Mateo says, so he steals my attention back. Instead of penetrating me right away, he brings his hands up to cover my breasts, giving them a squeeze. He catches one of my nipples between his fingers and pinches, sending jolts of pleasure through my core.

"Remember when you told me you liked being called a slut in the bedroom, little one? And I told you I'd remember that for when I fucked you?"

I narrow my eyes at him, since I can't be sure he didn't say that for Mateo's benefit. "And I told you we would *never* fuck? Yes, I remember that."

Rafe smiles. "You were wrong."

My heart thuds in my chest at his words, then sparks to life as he slides his cock inside me. I grab hold of the bedding beneath my fingertips, needing something to hold onto. I writhe as he pulls back and drives into me harder, drawing a helpless moan out of my body. Oh, god, the friction. He moves inside me effortlessly, every aggressive stroke so pleasurable I want to die.

He lifts my hips and thrusts deep, bringing his face closer until he's inches from mine. With him so close, I can't resist holding onto him instead of the bedding, so I rest my hands on his shoulders, looking up into his eyes as he thrusts inside me again and again.

"You feel me deep inside your pussy, little one?"

I nod my head.

"You want more?"

I nod again.

His voice is hard. "Say it. I don't care if he's watching, ask for it."

I turn my head, refusing without words. I won't do that. Not when I'm not even sure if Mateo is okay watching. He's behind me so I can't see him unless I tilt my head back and look, and I can't bring myself to do that when someone else is fucking me.

"Mia," Rafe says, firmly.

I meet his gaze again, still holding onto his shoulders. It makes my stomach sink to look into his face and deny him, but not as much as thinking I might hurt Mateo if I don't. "No. I'll ask for my husband's cock, no one else's."

Instead of becoming annoyed, his lips tug up in amusement. "You are the most loyal faithless little slut I've ever met."

I roll my eyes, wrapping my legs around his hips and tilting my pelvis, letting him get even deeper. "Just be nice to my husband so I can enjoy this."

Rafe chuckles, leaning in and trailing kisses along the curve of my shoulder. "I can probably do that," he murmurs.

I sigh with pleasure. "Good."

"We'd have more fun without him, you know."

"We'd never be doing this without him," I counter.

"You've been wrong before," Rafe reminds me, his mouth moving to the front of my throat. He leaves several hot kisses there, then gives me a little bite at the base of my neck. The nip surprises a little gasp out of me and I rub it.

"Did you just bite me?" I ask, eyes wide.

"Barely. Just a little souvenir. He'll fuck you a little harder the next few days when he sees it," Rafe offers, smirking faintly. "You can thank me later."

I bite back a smile. I can't complain about anything that urges my husband to fuck me harder, even if it is a love bite from someone else. "You're pushing it, Morelli."

"I'm playing nice," he promises, lifting my hips a little higher and sliding right up against my G-spot.

"Oh, god," I murmur, reaching overhead for purchase. He has me in the middle of the bed, so there's nothing to grab onto. Now that he's there, he stays there. I didn't think he knew where it was, but now as he pounds deliberately against the same spot, I think he was just enjoying himself first. I writhe helplessly, torn between the urges to come for him, and to get away. He doesn't give me a choice. He holds onto me, sliding his cock against that magical spot until I come apart beneath him, clutching at the bed and seeing stars.

I'm weak with physical release, so I don't fight him when he gathers me in his arms and nuzzles me close. I want to be close, too. I almost wish he could kiss me, just right now. Since he can't, I settle for nuzzling into his neck again, giving him a series of 'thank you' kisses.

I want a nap, but now Mateo joins back in, grabbing me and tugging me across his lap. I feel weird straddling him when Rafe was just inside me, but I guess since he wore a condom, it's okay.

Running his hands down my upper arms and leaning in to kiss my forehead, Mateo asks, "Have fun?"

"Did *you*?" I ask, since that's more important to me.

His lips curve upward, his eyes warming. He cradles my face and draws me close, brushing his lips against mine. "I always have fun when you're involved."

I smile back and wrap my arms around him, melting against him. "Is it stupid if I missed you?"

Now he chuckles, rubbing my back. "No, it's not stupid. You won't have to miss me anymore," he assures me.

"Good," I murmur.

He keeps me settled against his chest, but his hand slides between my legs. He uses the wetness he finds there to ready my ass.

"Change condoms."

"I'm working on it, boss," Rafe mutters.

I need to feel my husband, so I bury my face in his neck, leaving a trail of soft kisses along his skin. I want to make him feel good. I need unspoken reassurances. I want to ask questions, but I can't because Rafe is still here.

Instead, I lean back so I can look into Mateo's face. I keep one arm looped around his shoulder, but I run my fingers through his hair with the other, searching his eyes for some sign of how he's really feeling.

He knows exactly what I'm doing, so he shakes his head at me. "Would you relax? You've had three orgasms in just this session, for god's sake."

Smiling faintly, I said, "And you still manage to keep me on my toes."

"We'll have to work a little harder to wear you out," Mateo offers.

"What's next?"

Rafe comes up behind me, putting his hands on my shoulders. He drops a kiss at the nape of my neck, then says, "I do believe I'm going to fuck this pretty little ass while you ride your husband's cock."

My eyes widen slightly, but Mateo merely smiles. "Don't worry, you'll like it."

"You can't possibly be sure of that," I tell him.

"You will," Rafe offers, giving my shoulders another brief massage. "I know lots of girls who live for DP."

"See? Rafe knows lots of girl who agree with me."

"Notice how neither of you men, so sure I'm going to love this, possess a vagina? I've been on both your cocks now, and I don't see how this is going to be fun. I'm going to be so full I won't to be able to breathe."

"Or do anything else," Rafe tells me. "Your body will be completely at our mercy. You'll lose all control."

My ears perk up. "Really?"

"All of it," he verifies. "You'll be our toy in the most literal sense."

Oh, well, that doesn't sound terrible at all. Feigning nonchalance, I say, "Okay, we'll see how it goes."

Mateo grins, shaking his head at me and lifting me, repositioning me on his lap. Pleasure and relief mingle together as he fits his perfect cock inside me. I run my fingers through his hair, kissing him tenderly on the lips. The taste of his kiss soothes me and sets me on fire at the same time. I love kissing this man more than anything. I move my hips, riding him, but he grabs them after only a moment and steadies me. Pulling me forward, he places a hand on my back and watches Rafe. I tense a little when the wrong pair of hands grasp my hips and Mateo moves his to my waist.

I know this isn't going to be comfortable. Rafe and Mateo are comparable size-wise, and when Mateo has taken my ass, it's never been comfortable at first. So I'm prepared when Rafe pushes inside me and it doesn't feel magical. I wait for the invasion to start feeling good. I feel too full at first, Mateo in my pussy, Rafe penetrating my ass. Mateo picks up the pace first, giving it to me hard, just the way we both like. Rafe follows his lead at first, but once my ass is used to him and he's confident I can handle it, he fucks me like he wants to kill me. The savagery is unexpected—and coming from both ends, since Mateo is, well, Mateo.

I'm a fuckdoll in the most literal sense, being used hard by the two most dominant men I've ever known. Every nerve ending comes alive as their hands roam my body and their hard bodies support mine while they fuck me. Rafe was right that I can't do anything—my body goes wherever they want it to, does what they want it to do, takes whatever they dole out. It feels so damn good. I want to kiss my husband, but they're using me too roughly for kissing.

Pressure builds with their bruising thrusts and the loss of control that comes along with both of them using me. I'm drunk on it, leaning whichever way they move me. One minute I'm leaning into Mateo, the next I'm arching back against Rafe, his big hands moving around my waist and playing with my breasts.

Mateo drives into me while Rafe plays with my tits and I come hard. He continues to fuck me while I ride it out, but the wave of pleasure doesn't crash and dissipate—I'm stuck on it. Mateo isn't done, of course, so he keeps fucking me, Rafe keeps toying with me, and I keep coming.

"Oh, god, please." I lean my head back against Rafe's shoulder.

He's pressed firmly against my back, supporting my writhing body as his thumb brushes my nipple. "Please what, little one?"

I don't even know, it's just a set of words falling out of my mouth. Everything feels so good. I feel so good, but the pleasure starts to feel wrenching. It's supposed to end. I can't even think. Rafe pulls out and shoves back into me from behind and I fall forward, collapsing against Mateo.

"You okay?" Mateo murmurs, his strong arms tightening around my upper body.

"Oh, god," I murmur into his neck. His thrusts slow as he checks on me, but thank fuck. I needed a chance to come down. My hearts pounds so violently I half-expect it to just give out.

Rafe notices and slows down, too. "Is she okay?"

Mateo nods, gathering my hair off my neck. "I think she's just getting tired."

Rafe chuckles warmly. "Aww, poor little one, are we fucking you too hard?"

I look over my shoulder to narrow my eyes at him. "I can take everything you give me."

"Great," he says, cheerfully. "I can keep going, then."

I sigh, slumping forward on Mateo's shoulder, but I suck it up and push my ass back down on his cock. "Bring it on."

Rafe grins at me, looping an arm around my neck and pulling

me back so he can kiss the side of my face. "There you go, that's the spirit."

Mateo isn't going to quit if Rafe won't, so my overstimulated body gets tossed between them some more. Mateo makes me come again—I think, though it's hard to say if Rafe helped, since he keeps touching me all over and pounding my ass so hard I think I might break apart. When I come that time, I nearly cry real tears. The orgasm is so sharp it nearly hurts, pulling energy I don't have from my body. My pussy squeezes Mateo's dick, begging it to be done. He thrusts deep inside me and groans; the hot sensation of his release is glorious—not just because I'm pleasing my husband, but because it means he's done with me and I can finally lie down.

Rafe isn't done, but seeing that we are, he grabs my ass and uses it until he comes, too.

"Jesus Christ," I say, my weak arms giving out as I collapse against the pillow-top mattress. "Holy shit. Fuck."

Rafe snorts with laughter, resting a hand on his chiseled abdomen as he lies down beside me. "Little one has a mouth on her."

"You two could literally fuck someone to death; I'm just throwing it out there. You can't, because Mateo is never going to fuck another woman as long as he lives, but it is a thing I think you could feasibly do."

"Since I'm not tied down, I'll keep the suggestion in mind. If I ever try it, I'll let you know how it works out."

"Ugh," I mutter, burying my face in Mateo's arm. "I need to sleep for five days."

Smiling, he snakes his arm underneath me and pulls me snugly against him. "I anticipated as much. Your morning and afternoon are clear. You can sleep in as long as you'd like."

"Five days," I reiterate. "And I need water. Do you think Maria would be mad at me if I asked her for water?"

A devious little smile pulls at Mateo's beautiful mouth. "I could always tell Adrian to bring it up."

"Oh, my god. Adrian doesn't know about this, does he?" I cover my face with my hands.

"No, he doesn't know."

"Please don't tell him."

Rafe props himself up on the pillow behind me and smirks. "Why? He'll be jealous, won't he? He gets all the second husband duties and none of the sex; I get sex without duties."

"He would not be jealous," I say, a little defensively.

"I think he would," Rafe disagrees. "He doesn't like me anymore and all I've done differently is flirt with you in front of him."

"He just doesn't like anyone who causes him trouble. You have trouble written all over you," I point out.

Mateo's eyes glow with pleasure as he tells Rafe, "Adrian was her first choice, you know; you were second string."

Rafe's eyes widen and he points to himself. "I'm the second choice? After Adrian? Seriously?"

I shrug without apology. "Adrian is awesome. Plus, he could play much nicer with Mateo than you did."

"If he's so awesome, why didn't you suck his dick instead of mine?"

"He's married," I remind Rafe. "Also, I didn't ask for a threesome at all. But if I had to have one, Adrian would have been my choice, yes. No offense. I just need things to be nice for Mateo, even in a fantasy situation, and you're too... you."

"But Adrian isn't," he surmises.

"Adrian would have been more accommodating, but I don't think he would ever do this in a million years, married or not."

"Unmarried, he might have," Mateo offers.

"I'm not so sure. Anyway, I don't want him to know about this because aside from the possibility of him judging me, he would think it was a truly terrible idea," I say, with certainty.

Mateo's thumb brushes the base of my neck. It feels nice and I can't move anyway, so I close my eyes and leave him to it. It doesn't occur to me why, until he says, "I can't believe you bit my wife, you fucking dick."

I open one eye. I don't care enough about this to open both. "Did it leave a mark?"

"It's going to bruise," Mateo says.

"No biting wasn't one of your rules," Rafe points out, sounding entirely unapologetic. "I didn't kiss her on the mouth and I used a fucking condom. Speaking of which."

The bed moves and I glance back to see Rafe climbing off to discard his condom. It's the first look I got at his back, but Jesus Christ, he has some good-looking back muscles. My gaze drops to his well-formed ass, but he catches me looking and I look away.

"I saw that," he says.

"Shut up," I reply, burying my face in Mateo's side again.

Mateo sounds less amused as he says, "Don't throw that away." He shifts me and reaches over to the bedside stand, cracking it open and drawing out a plastic bag. I frown in confusion.

"What the fuck is that for?" Rafe asks.

"Put the condom in it."

Rafe just stands there, baffled. "What? Why?"

I don't get why either, so I look at him over my shoulder.

Realization dawns on Rafe's face and his jaw drops open. "Are you fucking kidding me? This is the first time I've fucked her. Unless my sperm can escape a condom and miraculously imprint over Vince's months after conception, I am *not* the father."

"Then you won't mind if I check," Mateo states.

71

Now I scowl. "Check what? I told you we didn't have sex in Vegas."

"I know you did, sweetheart," Mateo says patiently, as if explaining away something to Rosalie that she's just too young to understand. Still, he holds the bag out to Rafe.

"This is fucking ridiculous," Rafe states, but he rips the bag out of his hand anyway.

I'm tempted to pull out of Mateo's embrace, but I'm too tired. Still, I shoot him a dirty look because he's talking to Rafe like he thinks there's a chance he's the father of my baby, and I already told him Rafe only touched me with his hand. Unless his fingers are capable of impregnating a woman, there's no chance.

If he was planning to linger prior to Mateo springing a DNA test on him, apparently he's not now. Rafe pulls his clothes back on and leaves, telling Mateo curtly the *sample* is on the bedside table. He's nicer to me, but I understand why he's so annoyed.

Mateo looks down at me, running this thumb over my furrowed brow. "Don't look at me like that. I'm just being thorough."

"You don't believe me."

"I *do* believe you. I believe that *you* believe Rafe didn't have sex with you. But it's possible you don't remember."

I lift an eyebrow. "I think I would remember that."

He watches me for a moment, then says, "All right, but you didn't tell me he slept in the same bed with you that night, and he says you passed out. Since I got new information, I'm just making sure nothing happened that you didn't know about."

"You think the man who didn't want to have sex with me without a safe word may have raped me?" I ask, skeptically.

"No, I just..." Shaking his head, he says, "Don't worry about it. It has nothing to do with not trusting you, let's just leave it at that."

I don't much like it, but I know there's nothing I need to do about it either. If Mateo needs the peace of mind, there's little harm in letting him run a pointless test. I don't understand his argument, but I'm too tired to run around in circles with him. He's given my brain a hell of a workout today, and all I want to do now is curl up with him and sleep.

As if sensing my needs, he moves on. "How'd that stack up to your fantasy?"

"Well, it had the wrong third person," I point out. "I think it would have been a much different experience with Adrian."

"Better?"

"Different. Obviously I have no complaints about the physical satisfaction aspect, but with him, I think there would have been less head-butting with you. You've been there for my stories; you know the evolution of my Adrian fantasy. It's more of a partnership with you two. He and Rafe are different personalities so they aren't interchangeable. Rafe was a more dangerous third, even though Adrian is a more dangerous person in actuality. At any rate, now that we've actually done it, I think I'm going to retire that particular fantasy. My bedtime stories are just going to star us from now on."

Nodding in understanding, Mateo says, "Since you and Elise are going to be friends now, that's probably a good idea."

"She doesn't want to be my friend," I state, shaking my head.

"I don't care what she wants," he replies. "You want her for a friend, so she's going to be your friend."

I shake my head, pulling myself up to kiss him. "You're crazy, but I love you."

Rolling me on top of his body and securing his arms around my waist, he looks at me, his eyes unreservedly warm since it's just the two of us. "I'm glad you enjoyed yourself."

"Thank you for making me have all the orgasms."

Smirking, he says, "Anytime."

3

A PERFECT VALENTINE'S DAY

MIA

Once in a while, I'm sneaky.

Like right now. I creep barefoot across the marble floor of the master bathroom and sneak a peek into my bedroom.

My beloved husband is supposed to be getting ready for dinner. Instead, he's lying on the bed next to our sleeping baby girl. She fell asleep holding his hand; he didn't want to wake her up, so he stayed put. That's his official story, anyway. I think he just loves watching her sleep as much as I do.

Warmth washes over me looking at them together now. His face is so relaxed, so at peace, so happy—usually he only looks like that around me.

His brown eyes shift suddenly and narrow on my face. A faint smile tugs at the corners of his mouth and he says, "Can I tell you a secret?"

"Is the secret that we're going to lose our reservations because Annalise is holding my big, bad husband hostage?" I ask, giving up my attempt at spying and walking over to our bed, toward two of the most important fragments of my whole world.

"No," he says, then pauses. "Well, probably. But the secret was that you're not the least bit stealthy."

I look at Annalise's tiny hand, wrapped securely around Mateo's finger. God, I love that finger. I love that hand. I love every single inch of this man, and I've gotta say, with my newborn baby girl's tiny fingers wrapped around it, the love is reaching nearly painful levels.

Since we're clearly not going anywhere anytime soon, I climb on the bed and snuggle up on Annalise's other side, looking down at the tiny bundle that has brought so much additional joy into our life.

For Valentine's day, I dressed her in pink and white. Her little white onesie reads quite accurately, "My heart belongs to Daddy" and she has a pink bow on her tiny little head, resting on her soft, dark hair. Bunched up on her legs are little pink leg warmers with white polka dots. She's absolutely perfect. Just looking at her makes my heart swell up with love—not just for her, but for the man who gave her to me. The man I'm sharing my life with. The most impressive man I've ever met. God, I am a lucky woman.

I already feel all gooey, then I look across the bed and see him watching her again. He watches her all the time, like he's terrified she might blink out of existence if he looks away.

"Remember when you didn't want to have another baby?" I tease.

Mateo smiles faintly. "Once in a great while I have a truly terrible idea. You always fix it for me."

I push up on my hands and knees and crawl gently across the bed. I'm careful not to disturb Annalise as I crawl around to Mateo's other side, but I need to be close to my husband. The man is my favorite drug, and I need a little hit.

When I get there without waking the baby, I curl my legs beneath me and lean against my sexy husband, gently combing my fingers through his dark hair. "I love fixing your terrible ideas."

His free hand comes up to catch mine and he drags it to his chest, flattening my palm over my heart. "I love you."

Filling up with affection, I keep my hand on his heart and lean down to brush my lips against his. "I love you, too. More than anything. More than *everything*."

Sighing with contentment, his brown eyes meet mine. "How about we stay in tonight and we'll go out for Valentine's Day tomorrow night instead?"

"Fine by me," I say, easily. "We don't have to do Valentine's Day at all. I have everything I could ever want right here in this house."

Smirking, he says, "Cornball."

"Nope, it's just the truth. We have a night off, no one will bug us, we can relax, play with our babies, curl up and watch a movie or cuddle. I don't care what we do; as long as I get to spend the night with you, it's a perfect Valentine's Day. Annalise or Tristan might want to borrow my boobs from time to time, but other than that."

"As long as I get some time with your boobs, too."

Smiling and leaning down to give him another kiss, I say, "You get as much time with all of my naked body as you want. I've had three babies in three years; that doesn't happen because I'm depriving you of your husbandly rights."

"Well, to be fair, I was only responsible for two—" I cover his beautiful mouth with my hand to shut him up.

"Shh."

He moves my hand but his grip on my wrist tightens and he yanks me forward. I go easily, curling against his sexy body and getting lost in his kisses. My abundantly powerful husband can easily sweep me up in him and wipe out my ability to even think, but right now he's still holding Annalise's hand, so he keeps things calm. As much as I crave my husband, I crave the family time, too. It's a difficult balance, finding time for everyone when Mateo works as much as he does. I make sure to try to fill in any gaps with the kids—and Adrian helps, bless him—but there's only one Mateo.

Gently breaking the kiss, he settles me against his chest and rests his hand on my back, looking over to check on Annalise again.

"Do you like the outfit I ordered for her?" I ask.

"Sure. I'm much fonder of the little human inside it."

I squeeze him, sighing happily. "Me too. I can't believe we made something so beautiful."

"I believe you did. We'll have to wait until she does more than sleep to see if she got any of me."

"She's devastatingly beautiful—clearly she got that from you."

"Yeah, right," he says, warmly. "I can't be away from her very long without thinking about her—a little worried she got that from you."

"That's just because you're her daddy," I assure him.

"I don't know, West hangs around her every chance he gets."

"West is six," I state.

"Doesn't matter. She already pulls him in and she can hardly stay awake."

I shake my head against his chest. "You're crazy."

His tone is dry as hell. "Yes, because I'm wrong so frequently, I couldn't possibly be picking up on something you're not."

"I think maybe you're just not used to this feeling of protectiveness. It's scary, loving someone so much. Obviously you love all our children, but Annalise is the baby. The last one. And she *does* already show a strong preference for you over everyone else—even me, and I'm not only the family baby whisperer, but her only source of food. She would rather be snuggled by you than let go so she can eat, and that's not how babies usually work. She's already a daddy's girl. It makes sense that you're more paranoid about her."

"I'm not paranoid," he mutters.

"Not to mention, you've seen how much trouble I've stirred up over the years, and I was just some nobody. Annalise is your daughter. She's a Morelli." I prop myself up on his chest so I can look at him, and bring my free hand up to lightly tap his head. "She may have the power of this mind, the appeal of your name, and whatever odds and ends I managed to throw in there. She has all the ingredients to be a real force of nature."

"Like I said, it's going to be trouble."

"You think all our kids are going to be trouble. You insist that with literally every single one."

"Because they're all Morellis," he states. "It goes without saying they'll be trouble. Lily's the only one I'm not worried about. All the other kids will terrorize everyone."

I lift an eyebrow, since he's been so cocky about the importance of his genes before. "Well, that's your fault, not mine. And Dom isn't going to be any trouble. He's a little sweetheart. Did I tell you what he did the other day when—"

The door bursts open. To say this is not a regular occurrence would be an incredible understatement. No one ever opens our bedroom door and comes in unannounced, but suddenly Adrian flies in, uncaring of whether or not he's interrupting.

Mateo grabs my waist and pulls me off him, extracting his finger from Annalise's hand and leaving us here on the bed. His voice is much harder as he demands, "What's wrong?"

"We don't know where Bella is."

"What?" Mateo barks.

I glance beyond Adrian and see Lily in the hallway, twisting a lock of blonde hair over and over again, a nervous look on her face.

Adrian fills him in as quickly as possible. "Ju was just gathering all the kids for dinner. Bella isn't there. Ju can't remember when she last saw her. I went in the surveillance room and checked all the cameras; she's not in the house. I can start reviewing the tape to see when and how she left, but I thought I should come tell you now."

"Track her phone," Mateo says, simply.

A look of dread on his handsome features, Adrian says, "I did. The problem is, it's in her room. Wherever she is, she didn't take it with her."

Silence falls for a loaded moment, then Mateo says, his voice deadly calm, "My pre-teen daughter is missing and she doesn't have her *phone?*"

Nodding grimly, Adrian says, "That's right."

My stomach sinks and I push up off the bed. All the noise has Annalise stirring, so I scoop her up and settle her against my chest, walking past Adrian and Mateo toward Lily, still hanging back, watching the scene unfold fearfully. Fearful because Bella is missing, or fearful because she knows something?

As I come closer she backs up, and once we're out in the hallway alone, I ask quietly, "Do you know where Bella is, honey?"

Lily shakes her head quickly, her big blue eyes widening. "No."

"Where was she last time you saw her?"

"In her bedroom. She was writing something down—in a notebook, I think."

"Her diary?" I question, latching onto something that might hold clues.

"No, it wasn't her diary. Just a—a regular notebook."

"Do you know what she was writing? A letter? A list? Was it school work?

79

"I don't know what she was writing."

I don't believe her. Since she's still wide-eyed and nervous, I nod like I do. "Okay, honey."

I'm just about to head back in the bedroom, but Adrian nearly bumps into me as he storms out. Mateo follows behind him, shrugging on his suit jacket.

Mateo's gaze hits mine just as he's about to pass. "I'm sorry; I have to deal with this."

Glancing back at Lily once more, I follow, speeding up so I can catch up to Adrian. "Hey, slow down."

Adrian looks over at me, raising his eyebrows. "I can't *slow down*; I have to find your missing daughter."

He has a point, but I think there's something they're overlooking. Their damn Morelli instincts have shown one glaring blind spot in the past—they don't think about questioning women. They don't expect women to wreak havoc, to keep important secrets or sell each other out. You would think Mateo might have learned his lesson when *I* went missing because my own best friend sold *me* out, but here we are.

There's no reason I can see that Lily should have been following Adrian, but Mateo doesn't even question it.

I glance down at Annalise, sleeping peacefully against my chest, her little butt pushed out, supported by my hand. He's right; the girls probably *are* going to be all sorts of trouble—but only because he won't expect them to be.

No one taught Mateo how to raise sons and daughters; he was only taught to train potential employees and the women who would support and enable them. Bella was such a well-behaved child when I first met her—the perfect Morelli girl, quiet, appreciative, and out of the way. Obviously we've shaken things up in the years since; Annalise is never going to be five-years-old, sitting beside her formal, intimidating father, too timid to ask him to cut up her food—she's going to be sitting right in his lap, waving a meatball in his face and trying to feed him a bite.

Bella's still a good kid, but she's straddling the difficult line between being a little girl, and coming of age. I know Mateo is probably thinking the worst case scenario, that something horrible has happened to her, that she's been kidnapped by some rival force he's going to have to crush.

I don't think so, though. I think our well-behaved eldest daughter snuck out, knowing we weren't supposed to be home this evening. I think the Morelli daughters are already causing trouble, and he's not ready for it.

Mateo is cool and collected on the surface, but I can see his wheels turning as he falls into step beside Adrian. "Did you call Ethan?"

Adrian shakes his head. "He took Willow to Paris for Valentine's Day."

"Fucking Valentine's Day," Mateo mutters. "Why do we all have to love our wives?"

"Hire all bachelors from now on," Adrian says, lightly. "'Round the clock availability."

"I'm going to," Mateo states. I can't tell if he's joking.

"It's fine. I don't need Ethan; you know I'll find her," Adrian assures him, firmly patting his shoulder. "I just wanted to loop you in, that's all."

Mateo stops outside the study to dismiss me. "Why don't you go play with the kids while Adrian and I work on this?"

"I want to help," I tell him, stealing a glance back at Lily, who still lingers, watching us.

"I appreciate that, but you'll just get in the way."

My beloved husband takes me seriously as a co-parent and life partner, but when it comes to "business" he doesn't think I can hang. Something about me trying to save people and making extra work for him. Utter nonsense.

I cock an eyebrow at him. "Is that right?"

He leans in to kiss me, to smooth down any feathers he may have ruffled. "I didn't mean it like that. You'll distract me. I need to focus."

"Can I make a suggestion?"

"Sweetheart, time is of the essence right now."

I shake my head at him, leaning in to kiss him on that sexy mouth of his. "You're exasperating sometimes. Fine, go on, I'll talk to Adrian."

"I need Adrian," Mateo states, backing into the room. "Don't hold him up."

Given my husband's right hand man is slightly more capable of seeing the value in a mother's input, he hangs back. "What's up? You think of something I should know?"

Lily is behind me and I still need to scare the bejeezus out of her, so instead of showing my hand, I lean in close and whisper to Adrian, "Check Tommy's house."

Adrian scowls. I nod faintly. I'm no happier about it than he is.

Sighing heavily, Adrian says, "I'm not ready for this."

"No one is," I agree.

Now he storms into the study and I pull the door shut, falling back and nodding at Lily. "Come with me. I need a distraction while your father looks for Bella."

"All right," she says, trailing behind me as I head for the playroom.

She's still twisting her hair, a nervous habit of hers. I'm relieved she didn't pick up on what I told Adrian because after all I've lived through in this house, I have one firm lesson to teach: we don't keep secrets from Adrian, no matter who asks us to.

"How come you were following Adrian?"

Her cheeks flush. I don't know if it's because she has a bit of a crush on Adrian, or because she knows where Bella went and she feels guilty for lying. "I don't know. I just wanted to see if he could find her, I guess. Will she be in trouble?"

"She could be in serious trouble right now," I state, shaking my head and absently rubbing Annalise's back. "Even if for some reason she left the house on her own, it's incredibly dangerous that she doesn't have her phone or a guard with her. We have no idea where she went and she's out in the city all on her own. *Anything* could go wrong. She could get seriously hurt—or worse. Your father has a lot of enemies. There are some very bad people out there who wouldn't hesitate to hurt a member of his family just to hurt him."

I can see the conflict in her young, unguarded face. "But maybe she's not out in the city. Maybe she was going somewhere and it wouldn't be dangerous. Like, to a house or something. Maybe she's just with a friend. Maybe no one took her. Would she be in a lot of trouble when they find her?"

"The longer we don't know where she is, the more trouble she's going to be in." I look down at her again. "If you have any idea where she is, it's very important that you tell us. Even if Bella asked you not to. I know you want to keep her confidence, but this isn't a normal family, honey. There *is* danger out there for us. I went with someone I thought was a friend years ago, and it got me in so much trouble, I may never have seen any of you again."

"I remember," she murmurs lowly.

"The same thing could happen to any of us, and it may not end so well again. There's a reason Mateo is so protective of us. I know it may not always seem fun or fair, but he has to do it to keep us safe. If you know something, you need to tell an adult. Me or Adrian, in particular."

Lily is so uncomfortable, torn between not wanting to keep a secret from me and her loyalty to her best friend. I'm relieved it's loyalty to her best friend causing the conflict. That hasn't always been the case around here, and that's another page from the family history I don't intend on living through a second time.

As soon as Lily gets to the entry door of the playroom, she runs inside to get away from all the mom-guilt I'm piling on top of her.

Elise is already inside playing with the little ones, but when she sees me, she puts Candace down and rushes over for an update. "What's happening? Adrian bailed on dinner and he didn't give me any details, he just said Bella's missing?"

Since Lily is nearby, I lean in and tell her I think they have a lead, but I don't want to talk about it in front of the kids. She nods her understanding, sighs with concern, then drifts back toward the smallest ones.

A trio of babies sit on the soft mat, playing with blocks. Elise and Adrian's daughter, Candace, and my sons, Dom and Tristan. Dom is the eldest of the three, so he's the leader of their little construction crew. Tristan gnaws on blocks, Candace hands them to Dom, and he carefully stacks them on the tower. Candace gets intrepid sometimes and skips the line, but her motor skills aren't quite up to snuff, so she nearly knocks down the tower every time she stacks one herself. My little gentleman kindly steadies it for her and she claps with approval. They're so damn cute.

As soon as Dom sees me, he beams a smile up at me and holds up a block. "Here, mama."

"Thank you, baby," I say, gently dropping to my knees while I cradle Annalise. Once I'm seated and she's still sleeping, I take the block. "This is a great block. Do you know what color it is?"

"Red!"

I look up, since that was not Dom who answered me, but his slightly older brother, Roman. He toddles over and drops on his butt beside me, reaching for the block. "My block."

"That's not how you ask," I remind him.

Roman is not big on asking for things, he's big on taking them. Normal moms tell me not to worry, it's just his age, but since Mateo fathered him, I still find it worth worrying about.

"My block," he repeats, grabbing for it, but I pull it away.

Candace chimes in, reminding him of his manners. "Pease!"

Roman looks at her, but swiftly dismisses her and reaches for the block again.

I hold it up out of his reach. "Nope. What's the magic word?"

"Pease," Candace says again, not even watching at this point. She's too busy building a block tower with Dom. Tristan was helping them, but now that Roman is over here stirring up conflict, his little brother is just sitting there observing to see what happens.

Roman sighs and dramatically drops back against the floor, staring up at the ceiling. He can't even believe we won't all cede to his demands and deliver a mountain of red blocks at his little feet.

I can't help smiling as I ruffle his hair. He's so damn cute, and so very much his father's son. "Just say please and I'll give you the block, Roman."

He would rather live the rest of his life in a block-less world.

"All right," I say, with a warning tone. "Last chance. I'll give the block to Candace and Dom if you can't remember your manners."

"Stupid block," Roman mutters.

Well, I tried. Since I have to follow through, I hand the block to Dom instead.

"Thank you, mama," he says, placing it on top of the tower. Candace claps like he just finished constructing the Leaning Tower of Pisa.

Roman huffs and stands up. I expect him to wander away from us and go find something more fun to do where he won't have to say please, but instead he steps forward and kicks over the block tower.

Dom grasps the sides of his face, almost comically shocked. "Oh no!"

Candace scowls up at Roman. "Hey!"

"Stupid blocks," Roman announces, stomping past her.

"Hey, you come back here," I call after him.

He doesn't, but he doesn't make it far—Candace's older brother steps directly into his path, looking down at him with a none-too-pleasant look on his face. "Go tell Candace sorry."

"No," Roman says, stomping his foot.

Gripping the back of Roman's shirt, Westley Palmetto turns his little ass right around and urges him back toward Candace. "Tell Candace you're sorry for knocking over her blocks. She worked really hard on that tower."

"I wanted it," Roman complains. "My block."

"Say it right now or I'll smash your juice box," West says, his patience apparently at an end.

Still scowling, still with his little arms folded across his chest, Roman mutters, "Sorry, Candace."

"And Dom," West adds.

Roman looks up and gives West a dirty look, but then with another huff, he says, "Sorry, Dom."

Sighing with pleasure, Elise leans over and nudges me. "Aren't you glad you have my kids around to balance out Mateo's?"

Even though I absolutely adore my difficult husband, I can't help admitting, "Yes."

MATEO

There are a lot of things I excel at in life, roles I've studied and learned so well, you'd think I was born to play them. Ousting my asshole father and taking over his role in the family? Piece of cake. More than doubling my family's income through a variety of legitimate and not-so-legitimate ventures? I can literally do it in my sleep. Playing with human lives and manipulating them into doing whatever I want them to do, like they're literal puppets with carefully attached string? No problem. Keeping my inconveniently loving wife safe and happy, despite the many obstacles she's thrown in my path along the way? Sure, I can do that.

Raising a pre-teen girl, however, is not a job I was cut out to do. Ordinarily I let my wife do all the heavy-lifting here with Adrian stepping in to pick up any slack I don't have time to deal with. They say it takes a village, right? Well, I have a carefully chosen village around to take care of all that for me.

But tonight a 12-year-old girl managed to sneak past all my security and out of my house. Now she's god-knows-where, doing god-knows-what, with god-knows-who. Historically I wouldn't worry so much about the details—she's 12, after all—but Bella is my neediest child. I assume it's because she was my first, and when I had her, I hadn't a single clue how to raise a child. I assumed her mother would take care of that, but I picked out a shitty mother for her. Even before she died, she didn't show any signs of being very good at that particular role.

For the first several years of Bella's life, she didn't fare much better than I did, I guess. I didn't think about it at the time. I did the best I knew how. I hired a capable woman to be her nanny and take care of her, to do all the shit I didn't know how to do and didn't possess the time—or, if I'm being honest, the interest—in learning.

Bella was five by the time the family grew and the entire running of my household changed. Now she has a mother and a father, but those first five years left their mark. Despite being my eldest child, Bella is perhaps the least secure. The years of not making time for her didn't just disappear because she gets more attention now.

I shouldn't be surprised I managed to fuck up my kid. That's what parents do, even when they try—and for a long while, I guess I didn't know what trying meant.

Long story short, I really hope my 12-year-old isn't out getting pregnant right now because I was a shitty dad for a few years. I'll have to kill the little bastard, and if she is where Adrian thinks she is right now, that would be pretty bad.

The son of fucking cops. Well, the nephew of a cop, but I looked into it, and blue practically runs in this kid's veins. His uncle is Chicago PD, his grandfather is a retired chief of police, and he has an aunt who's trying to make detective.

All of them are the annoying kind—the ones who can't be bought. The noble assholes who would prefer to struggle and uphold their principles than take some extra cash and live an easier life just for looking the other way.

This little asshole is the last person in this entire city I want her to like, so of course this is the one she's been nurturing a crush on for years. I swear, she only likes this kid to spite me. I thought I had some time before I really had to worry about the little shithead, but right now I'm not so sure.

She's 12.

Even *I* wasn't fucking anyone when I was 12.

I'm going to put her little ass in a goddamn tower, mark my fucking words.

Adrian pulls into the driveway, looking every bit as unhappy as I am. It's not even his daughter potentially inside this house, but it may as well be. As he storms up the porch steps, he oozes more paternal outrage than me, and she *is* mine.

"No fucking solicitors," Adrian mutters, reading the little gold-plated sign on their front door as he presses the doorbell. "I'll show them fucking solicitors."

I give him a light pat on the shoulder. "Down, boy. Let's see if she's even here first."

"She better fucking be here," he blusters. "And she's grounded for a month if she is," he adds, in case I didn't know.

"Justine's birthday party is this weekend," I remind him. I'm not even sure why I remember when Ethan's daughter's birthday is, but I remember Mia saying they were going out to pick up a present for her.

"She's not going to any parties," Adrian states. "She's grounded. Grounded means no parties."

This is not my arena, so I shrug and watch a fuzzy shape approach the door through the frosted window.

"And no phone, either," Adrian adds, stacking up her punishment. "If she can't be bothered to have the thing on her when she sneaks out of the goddamn house, she doesn't get to have it."

I take a step to the side as the door opens. A big, burly man appears in the doorway and narrows his eyes at me. I can tell by the instant distaste on his face that he obviously knows who I am, and by his lack of surprise that he must know why I'm here.

Like he doesn't, he says, "Correct me if I'm wrong, but I do believe my wife told yours that you aren't welcome on our doorstep."

His wife better not have said that to my fucking wife. If she did, Mia certainly didn't tell me about it. "Is my daughter—who is very clearly a minor—in your house right now?" I ask.

The man responds with a deeply stubborn chin-lift. "So what if she is? Little girl needs some positive influences in her life."

"Get the fuck out of the way," Adrian says, apparently beyond civility.

"You step one foot inside my house, I'll call the police. The only member of your family welcome over that threshold is that little girl, and only because I'm not going to fault her for who her father is."

I roll my eyes. "How noble of you. Go get my daughter or *I'll* call the police myself and have you charged with attempted kidnapping."

Barking with laughter, he says, "That's rich, isn't it?"

"I'm a shameless bastard; trust me, I'll do it," I tell him.

"Why don't you have her mother call and tell me to send her home?" he asks, before theatrically smacking his palm against his forehead. "Oh, wait; you murdered her mother, didn't you?"

Offering him an icy smile, I draw my phone out of my jacket pocket and unlock it.

"He's not bluffing," Adrian informs the bastard. "He will legitimately have the cops show up on your doorstep. We'll all have to fill out paperwork and waste taxpayer dollars. It'll be a real hassle —and that's just tonight. I can't begin to imagine the kind of bad luck that might start to befall you after we leave here tonight."

Narrowing his eyes at Adrian, he says, "You threatening me?"

"Of course not," Adrian says, smoothly. "Just observing that sometimes when people become a problem for us, things start to go wrong for them. Damndest thing."

I know he's pissed off, but I really don't want Adrian threatening the family members of starchy police officers with violence, so I open up the keypad of my phone and press in a 9. "This is going to be a funny story. We're all going to look back and laugh about the time Mateo Morelli showed up on your doorstep and called the cops on *you*."

"Police officers," he says, rather icily. "Not cops."

"I could give a fuck less," I state, losing my smile.

He holds my stare for another moment, but then he slams the door shut and his shape disappears back the way it came.

"I hate these fucking people," Adrian mutters.

"Yes, they're not my favorite, either."

"We should transfer Bella to a different school, get her away from this little asshole once and for all."

I roll my eyes at the ridiculousness of such a suggestion. "I'm not going to run from them. If the asshole father keeps pissing me off, I'm going to buy the company he works for and have him fired. Maybe *they'll* move."

"I'd rather break his fucking face," Adrian states.

"If I fuck with this family, I'd prefer to use legal measures. They're rigid, law-abiding citizens; don't want to give them anything to use against me." I look at Adrian as a new idea occurs to me. "We should look into the wife. Maybe hire someone to seduce her. See how smug the asshole is when his wife's running around on him."

Adrian shakes his head. "You're so mean."

My eyebrows rise. "You just wanted to break his face three seconds ago."

"Yeah, but you want to break his heart and ruin his life."

"Damn right; the impression will last longer. I'm gonna look into buying that company. Even if I don't play that card now, could be a nice one to have up my sleeve later."

"We have very different ways of solving problems," Adrian states.

"Mine's pretty effective," I point out.

Raising his scarred knuckles to show me, he says, "So is mine."

The door opens again, and this time my daughter is on the other side. The brawny asshole has a giant hand resting on her shoulder like he's going to protect her, but of course he has no choice but to surrender her to me, since I'm her fucking father.

I'm pretty sure it's just to be an asshole that he tells her, "You're welcome here anytime, Bella."

"Not without permission, you're not," Adrian states, reaching forward and grabbing her shoulder, ushering her out of the house and onto the porch with us.

Bella looks up at me, her cheeks flushed with anger or embarrassment—I'm not sure which.

"Go to the car," I tell her.

Bella shakes her head at me, her eyes glistening with unshed tears, before storming down the porch steps. Adrian follows after her, but I remain on the porch with Tommy's father.

Once I hear the car door shut behind me, I speak. "Let me make myself very clear. I don't care what you think about me. That doesn't matter." Pointing back at the car, I state, "*That* is *my* daughter. My little girl. And if anyone in your family ever helps her sneak out of my house again, you and I are going to have a problem. If your son lays a *finger* on my daughter, we're going to have a problem. Basically, drawing my daughter any further into your family than you already have is a very ill-advised idea that I would strongly urge you to reconsider. I'm hoping this is a little blip of a crush that Bella outgrows before long, but if you have it in your head that you're going to 'rescue' her and turn her on me, know that I will put a stop to it."

"Sounds like you're threatening me, Mr. Morelli."

God, I hate the sound of his smug voice. "I am," I state. "If you or any member of your family crosses me, I will rip your life apart —and I won't break a single law to do it."

His withering glare is heavy with hatred, but I'm done here. I've said my piece. I turn my back to him, make my way down the steps, and return to my Escalade. Adrian glares at the man as he holds the door open for me, then slams it shut once I'm inside, undoubtedly continuing to glare at him as he walks around to the driver's seat.

I look over at my daughter, sitting in the seat beside me with her arms crossed tightly over her chest, her face turned toward the window instead of looking at me.

"What were you thinking?" I demand.

She shakes her head again, too overcome with emotion to form any words.

"You can't sneak out like that, Bella. We've never stopped you from coming over to Tommy's house. Why didn't you just ask?"

"Because you always make me take someone," she bursts out, turning to vent her feelings at me. "You don't let me go alone. I don't want Uncle Alec or some goon sitting outside waiting for me. It's like I'm a prisoner! I wanted to have dinner with Tommy's family because they're *nice*. Because they're *good*. They're everything you're not!"

Wow.

Her breath hitches and she angrily swipes tears from her

cheek. "I just wanted to spend tonight with people who *care* about me."

That is an insane, stupid thing to say. Telling her that probably won't help. "Your family cares about you," I state. "You aren't some unloved little waif, Bella. Come on."

"You just don't get it," she says, shaking her head.

"You're right, I don't. So explain it to me."

"No," she snaps, turning back to the window. "You humiliated me! Why would you show up on his doorstep like that? You know how Tommy's family feels about you. And do you know how stupid that made me look?"

I can only stare at her. "You snuck out of the house without so much as a cell phone, Bella. I didn't know where you were. You could have been hurt."

"Like you care," she mutters.

Closing my eyes, I massage my temples. I'm just about parented out right now. Twelve-year-old girls are too irrational for me to deal with.

I draw my phone back out of my pocket to message Mia. I need to fill her in and warn her that I'm bringing home a hot mess of emotion. This is Mia's wheelhouse. She's the one who deals with the meltdowns. I need a fucking drink.

Bella sniffles and pouts the whole way back. Adrian talked a big game on the way over about the piece of his mind he was going to deliver, but as soon as she dissolved into tears, he went quiet. Fucking softie.

I am quite happy to deliver my daughter into the capable hands of my wife as soon as we get home. Since I texted ahead to let her know what she would be dealing with, she is waiting in the foyer to receive Bella as soon as she storms inside.

Grown-ass men I can control, but for a 12-year-old girl, I need my wife.

94

She needs to be yelled at, but instead Mia opens her arms, bringing Bella in for a hug. She squeezes her and tells her how worried we all were. I want to tell her how grounded she is, but Mia doesn't seek my input right now. With her arm around Bella, she ushers her down the hall, head bent like they're already talking.

Sighing heavily, I look over at Adrian. "Well, that was fun."

"I need a drink," he tells me.

I can't help smirking. "You read my mind."

I lead the way to my study and pour us each some Scotch—the old, expensive stuff. Tonight calls for it. Adrian accepts his glass and sinks into a wing chair. Since it's just the two of us, I take a seat in the one across from him.

"I'm glad this last one was a girl," I tell Adrian, before taking a sip.

His eyebrows rise with surprise. "Why? Because you're dying to do this again?"

"Because now we can stop," I correct. "Mia wanted a daughter so badly. If it had been another boy, I would've wanted to die. I would've had to keep going until she got a girl."

Rolling his eyes, he says, "Oh no, you would have had to impregnate your beautiful wife again? It's a hard life for you, isn't it?"

I take a sip, nodding even though he's not serious. "You should feel bad for me."

"I feel bad for all of us," he states. "This is just the start. Bella's the easiest kid you have, and she's already giving me gray hair."

"You do not have gray hair."

"I will, at this rate," he states.

I shake my head. "Don't worry so much. Bella's a good kid. Mia will straighten her out tonight. She's good at this kind of thing."

"That fucking family pisses me off. Watch her grow up and marry that little asshole."

"Over my dead body," I state. "Anyone who causes me this much annoyance is temporary, I promise you that."

"It's been, what, three years? That's a long time to nurse a dead-end crush."

"She's just a kid," I tell him.

"She won't be for too much longer," he warns me, seriously. "She's growing up, Mateo. Her needs are changing. You're her father; you have to rise to meet them. You heard her in the car. She needs more effort from you."

"She was just throwing a tantrum."

"No, she was telling you how she feels," he disagrees. "It's not enough to let everyone else deal with her. You've gotta do some fathering there and fix it yourself so she doesn't feel that way anymore. She'll be wide open for some little asshole to take advantage if she's got a void like that. Mia can do her best, but you're the one who needs to step it up."

I sigh, sinking back into the chair. "Tonight was supposed to be nice. I was supposed to be relaxing with my wife, thinking about the Tuscan sun and Mia in a bikini. Why can't Roman be an adult already? I need a break."

"The Tuscan sun?" he asks, cocking an eyebrow at me.

I nod, taking a sip of my drink. "I bought a house in Tuscany. A big villa right on the sea. I was going to give it to Mia for Valentine's Day."

His brown eyes widen. "You're giving her a fucking *house* for Valentine's Day? Jesus Christ, I just bought Elise a couple tickets to a play and some earrings."

Smiling faintly, I remark, "Might want to add some flowers, at least."

"Sure, that's basically the same thing as a house in Italy."

"It's a big house, you can come stay with us," I offer. "Mia said you want to retire to a beach house, too."

"I've spent enough of my life living under your roof; I should probably have my own by the time we retire."

"Nah, stay with us. More fun that way."

"Yes, you're so much fun," he says dryly.

"We're going to fly out for a week or so next month to check it out," I tell him. "Mia's birthday trip this year. You and Elise should join us."

"No offense, but I'd rather vacation with Ethan than you. I get enough of you on a day-to-day basis."

I shrug. "We can invite them, too. Hell, we can even invite Sal and Francesca. Make it a whole family affair—why not? It's a big house; there's plenty of room for all of us."

"Yeah?" he asks, a bit skeptically. Nodding slowly as he goes through it in his head, he says, "Maybe we could do that. Then I could at least tell Elise she gets a *week* in Italy. That's a pretty good gift."

"Sure, dress it up. Package it all together—a couple sundresses, a new pair of sandals. Put a little note inside saying you can't wait to see her wear them in Tuscany. Boom, you won Valentine's Day."

"Damn, that's a good idea. You're so good at gift-giving."

"I have a lot of practice," I point out.

After we shoot the shit for a little while, there's a light knock on the study door. I look up and see my lovely wife stepping inside, her arm around Bella's shoulder. Gone is the emotional mess I handed off to her. Now Bella is bright-eyed and smiling. Mia has worked her magic.

Feeling a lot lighter, I sit forward. "There are my girls."

Bella beams a little brighter. Mia's eyes warm with approval. "We're all better now," Mia says.

"Am I still grounded?" Bella asks.

"Yes," Adrian answers.

Bella shoots him a dirty look, but Mia ushers her over toward me. Releasing Bella, Mia takes a seat on my lap. I put my drink on the side table and wrap an arm around her waist, pulling her close and giving her a lingering kiss.

"I believe you and I have a bedroom to get back to," I tell her.

"About that," Mia says, rubbing my shoulder and leaning in to drop another kiss on my lips. She's trying to butter me up. She's about to say something she doesn't expect me to like. "How about instead of a quiet night in, just the two of us... we go out?"

I lift an eyebrow. "You want to go out *now*?"

"Not for dinner. But maybe we could stop somewhere for ice cream. Bella wants to go to the movies."

"Isn't she grounded?" I ask, hiking up an eyebrow.

"Starting tomorrow, yes," Mia says, glancing at Adrian as if to reassure him she didn't undermine his punishment. Looking back at me, she continues, "But tonight... ice cream and movie date, just the three of us. What do you think?"

I think I would like to haul my wife back upstairs and resume the relaxing evening we agreed upon before Bella's shenanigans robbed me of peace, that's what I think. I think we shouldn't reward bad behavior, and we should send her little ass up to her room—I don't know why Mia thinks ice cream and a movie is an appropriate response to Bella sneaking out of the house, going over to that little punk's house, and ruining everyone's night.

Of course, if Mia never rewarded bad behavior, she wouldn't have married me. When she senses someone needs her, she tends to overlook their unloving behaviors and fill their void, whether they ask her to or not. I should probably defer to her judgment on this particular issue.

Looking from Mia's hopeful face to my daughter's even *more* hopeful face, I know my peaceful night is canceled regardless. If I send Bella to her room, Mia will feel bad all night. Adrian was just saying I needed to step it up and do more shit like this anyway, and he probably has a point.

It wasn't the plan, but I guess I might as well embrace it.

Looping my free arm around Bella's waist, I tug her against my side and kiss her on the forehead. "Sounds like a perfect Valentine's Day to me."

THE END

ABOUT THE AUTHOR

Sam Mariano loves to write edgy, twisty reads with complicated characters you're left thinking about long after you turn the last page. Her favorite thing about indie publishing is the ability to play by your own rules! If she isn't reading one of the thousands of books on her to-read list, writing her next book, or playing with her adorable preschooler... actually, that's about all she has time for these days.

Feel free to find Sam on Facebook, Goodreads, Twitter, or her blog—she loves hearing from readers! She's also available on Instagram now @sammarianobooks, and you can sign up for her totally-not-spammy newsletter HERE

If you have the time and inclination to leave a review, however short or long, she would greatly appreciate it! :)

Made in the USA
Middletown, DE
05 June 2023